Raw Ne

edited by Brian

Willis

This is number _____7_____ of a 500 Limited Edition.

This book was first published in April 2002 by

RazorBlade Press

108 Habershon St

Splott

Cardiff

CF24 2LD

WALES

ISBN 0953146863

Printed and set in the UK.

A record for this book resides in the British Library.

Contents

Fiction

Other

Introduction

Sick Puppies

Right, now we've got your attention...

Raw Nerve (the original incarnation) had the sort of turbulent history that any publication in the horror genre, surely, would envy. We're not talking here about irregular deadlines, troublesome printers and a gadfly approach to the conventions of proof-reading - such things are common currency in the small press (though rarely all at once) and contribute little to garnering a loyal readership. No, *Raw Nerve* got one up on the competition by managing to raise its head far enough above the genre parapet as to attract fire from The Meejuh.

"A sick, shocking and dangerous magazine" - The Western Mail.

(Need I add at this point that Mr Darren Floyd has been dining out on this particular bit of journalistic hyperbole for rather too long now? And that his current co-editor is still rather miffed at the fact that the writer of that piece didn't mention any of *his* stories? I mean, who's a guy got to fuck...)

Comments such as the above didn't hurt sales, of course. This served to mollify those of us disturbed by the treatment given by the Western Mail to the whole (non-) issue; the editor had seen fit to place the story on the front page adjacent to pictures of the funeral of a child killed in the slaughter at Dunblane, which had happened only a matter of days previously. Some of us wrote letters to said editor protesting this distasteful

piece of 'low-blow' reportage; they were not printed.

The problem was, that *RN* had been getting a small remittance from the Welsh Arts Council back then, not much you understand, but enough to keep the production values reasonably high and the editor's blood pressure reasonably low. In the aftermath of such publicity, however, the funding was pulled (sorry, 're-prioritised') quicker than you could say 'let's get back to milking Dylan Thomas for all the bugger's worth'.

There was also, subsequently, the matter of Darren's appearance on a Radio Wales afternoon show hosted by a person called Mal Pope, during which both the host and his sidekick (some ludicrous little twerp whose name, mercifully, escapes me) alternated between patronising condescension and outright hostility. Darren coped with his usual good humour and aplomb, but it was, to all intents and purposes, an on-air ambush, carried out with all the subtlety and even-handedness of a Patriot missile descending on a Baghdad hospital.

The reason I mention all of this is to put this current reincarnation of *RN*- or should that be *resanguination*?- in some sort of perspective. It got us noticed, oh my, yes, even if some of that attention was rather less than positive (but then, that goes with the territory). Having attracted the attention, however, the problem arises of how to keep it, without falling into the trap of repeating ourselves or succumbing to shrill self-parody.The title of this piece is taken from the SFX review of *Razorblades,* the 'Best of *RN*' anthology published in 1997, which opined that 'there are some sick puppies in them thar hills'. And that's

fine, so long as it's clear that the magazine's purpose has not been merely to alert the world to the sickness of Welsh puppies, but to give those puppies a chance to crap on the lawn of the literary establishment. This may seem a tad juvenile, but here in Wales, where culture is still synonymous with dead pisshead poets and Bardic mummery, it's the sort of thing that can still get you on the front page of the papers.

This is why *RN* has lain fallow all this time; to allow Razorblade Press to consolidate on the audience it gained through the magazine and build itself up into the BFS-award winning fixture of the UK horror scene that it has become (There, Darren, I've mentioned the bloody award, now will you get your knee out of my spine?).

Besides, you wanted it back, didn't you? That's what you kept telling us, at any rate.

So here it is, albeit in a slightly different format (one that means we can get distribution through Proper Bookshops this time around, and don't have to rely on the sort of 'specialist' establishments that hide their copies behind a stack of The Comic Book Price Guide, and then inform us, with the tinge of regret in their voice, that they're just not shifting. Well, *duh...*). Thanks are due to all the contributors, particularly in light of their patience in waiting to see their stories in print, and to everyone who has inquired after the health of *Raw Nerve*.

As you can see, none of you need worry. It's as sick as ever it was.

Brian Willis 2002

The Sound Of Music In Hell

Rhys Hughes

Down there, the grim folk rush onwards, lips tight, eyes dark. There are no lamps in the street, but the windows of tall buildings burn brightly. There is no wind, but the rumble of thunder behind this or that block of offices shakes hats off heads, stirs dust and newspapers in the gutters. A large black cloud, streaked with veins, moves stealthily down the next avenue and rains blood onto heads...

The figures scatter, they find refuge in doorways. The cloud drifts on, channelled by the buildings. It is gone. The reemergence is slow but builds acceleration: faces peep, feet test the depth of crimson puddles. Once more the thoroughfare is full. They hurry. They grasp their bundles closer to themselves, looking about.

A manhole cover explodes high into the air, clatters to the ground, rolls down a hill. A trio of demons takes flight, crusted with the filth of the sewer, ochre eyes smouldering, gnashing carnelian teeth. Swooping on a man who tries to bat them free, they tangle their claws in his hair and strain to lift. They are not strong enough. The man topples, pulling the demons down. They spin in the blood, grappling, wrestling. One demon is crushed beneath its prey and groans, snaps and gives a last howl that fades to a chuckle, a cough, a sigh.

Its companions disengage, circle higher and swoop again. The man is still on the ground, attempting to rise. A demon perches on his back and he abandons the idea, crawling for the security of a market-stall. Claws hook his feet, but he is determined. He presses under the stall, a wagon selling pens and inks, his breath coming in sickening gasps. The cheated demons snap furiously at each other.

The man has abandoned his bundle in the middle of the road. A crowd gathers in a circle, peering at it enviously, but none are daring enough to venture close. A demon takes advantage of their caution. It hops over to the packet, seizes it, ascends up to the cavern roof and scatters the contents. There is fighting as the mob rush forward. Fists and boots are employed, also knives, chains, axes.

The demons retire to their sewer. Clouds of sulphur boil around the open manhole. Their giggles are heard under the asphalt, moving down and away. Below the wagon, the man sobs.

Elsewhere, trade resumes as normal: "Here!"

The whisper is keen. Its owner, dressed in an opera cloak, crouches in the dusk of an alleyway. He is furtive, eyes narrow. His hair sprouts from a single point on the top of his head in a matted geyser. Small but rubbery, his face betrays signs of former luxury. "Newcomers, eh? You'll need one of these. At a reasonable rate too. A real life-saver." Holding up a book, he breaks into a guffaw. In green lettering on the cover: New Harvard Dictionary of Musical Terms.

"Hey, come back!" he hollers as his prospects recoil. "I don't want your cash, just your handkerchiefs. You won't buy anything with money in our economy. It's barter or starve!"

He scowls, considers following them, changes his mind. He holds out his hand, palm upward, buttons the flapping wings of the cloak together. He peers into a storm-drain, checking his system of underground mirrors. Another blizzard is due, a vile one.

Just time for a quick supper...

"Well, think about it!" he calls after them, waving his book. "Yes, go for a walk. Clear your brains. We'll meet again, I'm sure." His voice becomes a mumble. He moves deeper into the alley. Here are dustbins, one of them being his larder. But which one? He has forgotten. He gropes for the nearest, tugs off the lid and jumps in alarm before licking his lips with a blistered tongue. The bin is full of eyeballs. They overflow onto the ground, staring unblinkingly at their surroundings. A pair of female orbs makes a crazy roll for freedom.

"Not so fast!" He blocks their escape with his foot. Hell is packed with surprises, some of them nice...

Well, eyeballs are a change from maggots.

"What has happened to us?"

"No idea. We've gone mad. Or maybe it's just me."

"I don't believe so."

They sit on a park-bench under a statue of an umbrella, both atop a mound. Ringing the mound is a system of standing stones, a cromlech. And around this swirls a snowstorm. All outside is violence, chaos, tempest. But here, below the parasol, quiet reigns.

"Right, Simon, let's get a grip. Let's try to remember what we were doing. Where were we before we came here?"

Simon frowns, battling with wisps of memory. His hand completes the motion it had started before this, but it seems lighter now. There is an acrid taste in his mouth, a strange fruit.

He clicks his fingers. "In the Hell's Bells, Petersfield. A pint of ale in my fist. Yes, I was drinking at a table in a corner. You had just selected a record on the juke-box and was coming over to join me. Then I felt peculiar, my skull seemed to expand."

"What happened next?"

Simon clears his throat. He runs a hand across his brow. Huge drops of sweat fly off at tangents. "How?"

"I'd rather know: where? Why is the sky made of stone? Are we in an underground cavern? Are we in Hell?"

The blizzard abruptly stops. Men and women caught out in it, frozen in their tracks, are quickly assailed by people who chisel their bundles from reluctant, icy grips. Fingers snap and clink like icicles. Then the windows of an adjacent building fracture all at once, raining daggers of glass on living and dead, shearing through the warmer bodies, shattering the cold ones, who tumble in blocks.

"I think," says Simon, after a pause, "that Hell isn't a bad guess. It's certainly a diabolical set-up."

Maddie sighs. The snow is already melting to muddy slush. The waste turns to water and sweeps down the alleys, diluting the puddles of blood and depositing all the debris into the storm-drains, making a grotesque, suggestive sucking noise. Soon everything is cleaner but far darker. The blanket of snow had reflected the only illumination: the burning windows of the buildings. The stone ceiling is lost in gloom, save for the veins of sparkling quartz which streak it. At regular intervals these give way to round hatches blushing with rust.

"So we're in Hell? But I thought we'd led reasonable lives. Did you try things you never told me about?"

Simon shakes his head. "We shouldn't be here."

"Look!" Maddie points out a man who is approaching. He walks with a stooping gait, poking at discarded pieces of paper with a pointed stick. He is muttering to himself. He seems almost normal, but his face lacks a full quota of parts. He climbs up the hill to the bench without looking, pauses by the statue of the umbrella and fumbles with his fly. Observing the couple for the first time, he restrains himself, weighing his member in one hand, his stick in the other.

"Hello there!" he drools. "Maybe you'd care to hand over your work? Unless, of course, you relish the prospect of transfixion." He scratches a scurvy nose with the wooden point.

Simon stands and adjusts his coat. "Enough of this foolery! I won't have it. Who are you? Where are we?"

"Newcomers? I should have been able to tell. You aren't yet dressed in rags. But you're the first arrivals we've had in nearly a week. I was beginning to think they'd mended the juke-box."

"Juke-box? What do you mean..."

"Green David's responsible. Nasty piece of work, he is. Burns holes in his teddy-bear with a cigarette. Listen, I don't want to gossip here. It's too dangerous a place to rest."

Leaving his organ still exposed, the hunchback staggers out through the perimeter of the stone circle. Maddie and Simon glance at each other for a moment before catching him up.

They stand on the pavement now, watching a disaster. Rubble pours from a hole in the ceiling, rapidly building a cone at the junction of two busy streets. A few arms and legs protrude at odd angles from the base of the pyramid. Maddie and Simon follow the hunchback across the tarmac, closer to the source of the catastrophe. At last he turns to them and chuckles, spattering them with vermiculous spittle.

"I'm going to dash for the scores. Keep my rivals off and I'll look after you. Otherwise you're on your own."

He springs towards the shower of rocks. His progress is observed by others, who loiter on the lips of the pavements like albino vultures. He dips in low, spears the bundle in the shirt pocket of one of the crushed corpses and rolls away to safety. A boulder narrowly misses his shoulder and he rises as nonchalantly as possible.

Suddenly, his observers are in pursuit, wailing like goats tortured over a low hedgehog. They overwhelm him and seek to snatch his prize. He struggles valiantly to keep the bundle under his body. Now there are two truncated mounds side by side, both growing, the first fabricated from a selection of minerals, the second from wasted torsos and flailing limbs. Only the hunchback's ulcerated member is still visible, through a gap in the scuffle which nobody is keen to fill.

Maddie nods at Simon. "We've got nothing to lose."

Each gripping a chunk of quartz which has cascaded onto the pyramid and bounced aside, the pair wade into the fracas, cracking heads with an enthusiasm which rapidly becomes an efficiency. Weakened by malnutrition and unknown torments, the pallid zombies offer little resistance. Femurs snap easily, like planks of frozen mucus.

The rubble stops pouring from the sky and a rapid change comes over the first stack. The larger stones settle at the circumference, rotating to an upright position. On the summit, a granite umbrella sprouts like a toxic mushroom. Immediately beneath the spotted cap, an embryonic bench, also igneous, strains through the gravel.

Maddie levers their new friend out from the heart of the undulating mass and they hasten away, down a random selection of lanes. Pausing for breath in a shop doorway, they exchange ambiguous gestures. There are no pursuers. The hunchback lifts his bundle.

"I need a safe place to study this."

Simon cranes for a closer view of the parcel. "How about a bench on another mound? They seem peaceful zones."

"Those are the most vicious spots in the city. You were lucky. Your umbrella was dozing after lunch. Didn't you notice the gristle and teeth scattered on the grass? It's not an amenity but an organism, a Municipal Persontrap. They don't have them on top, but they're proliferating at an astonishing rate down here, generating spontaneously from the dark humus which drops from the ceiling. We witnessed the origin of one just now. I don't want to be macerated by a parasol."

"Alright then, what lies beyond the urban limits?"

"Hell is like Swansea, without the poetic pretension. Don't attempt walking past the outskirts to the hills."

"Why not? Are they alive with the sound of music?"

The hunchback titters. "Just alive."

Maddie steps out of the doorway, only to be knocked sprawling by an injured demon which struggles to take off. Torn wings flutter like flags trodden in battlefield mud. Loose fangs rattle in blistered sockets. The yellow gaze of the being is clouded, pupils narrowed to slits. Something is wrong with its scales: they move unnaturally, bulging outwards with a splitting noise. The demon whistles mournfully through its lips, ballads of loss and despair. Then it collapses in a shuddering heap, draped over a fire-hydrant moulded like a blown nose.

"What happened to it?" cries Maddie.

"Victim of a parasitic fork, I presume. One of Green David's silver service jokes. They grapple with devils and lay their eggs in the liver. When the eggs hatch, the larvae jab their way out. Some demons enjoy it, or so I've heard. Cutlery is generally to be avoided in Hell. Stand back now, this beast looks close to bursting."

Maddie rejoins Simon, who is cowering behind the hunchback. Closing their eyes, they hear a momentous pop. The demon's abdomen has exploded, showering them with leathery shards, leaving it a deflated shell. Maddie is the first to risk a look. A thousand tiny tridents lie on the ground, flexing and cooling. Others clatter from the wound, dripping with ichor. Slowly these stand upright, finding their balance, moving their embossed tines in unlikely rhythms, marching away.

Once more Maddie steps onto the pavement. Again she is pressed back into the doorway, this time by a sudden rush of people. A mob are racing past, a seamless flow of rotten humanity. The hunchback pounds his stick furiously against bobbing skulls, but the barrier is impenetrable. Simon is bewildered by the velocity and frenzy.

"What's going on? What are they running from?"

"From? Oh no! What an opportunity I've missed! Person of importance has just died. His manuscripts are there for the taking." With a grimace the hunchback squats in the damp shadows.

The onslaught shows no signs of slackening. Simon turns and tugs at the door of the building. Before he can force it open, he feels the stab of the hunchback's spear in his appendix.

"But if we can't get out onto the pavement..."

"Don't even think about it. They may look like buildings from here, but inside it's a different story. They lead to gaps in reality. Best to stick with the street. We'll sit it out."

Simon shrugs. The trio wait for the crowd to subside, then gingerly emerge from the doorway. They proceed in the direction taken by the mob, but by the time they gain the source of interest there is little to see. Merely what they take to be a naked body.

Spread over a large area...

The hunchback pokes about for a minute, uncovers a trampled pair of extrovert spectacles. Further down the road, an artificial scalp of poor design. Both are clotted with waxy blood.

"Recognise him?" Maddie picks up a weak jawbone, a lip curved in an insincere smile, five talentless fingers.

"Only by rectum. He was a candle in the wind."

Dropping the scalp in distaste, Maddie wipes her thumbs on Simon. A ribbon of paper spirals from the lining of the toupee and tangles in her hair. Combing it free with the broken spectacles, she regards it warily. A crotchet winks at her from a shorn stave, a solitary note. "I think it is time we knew exactly what's going on."

The hunchback smirks. "Formal introductions first?" When Maddie and Simon nod in agreement, he indicates the end of the street. "We can talk as we move. Mustn't linger in one place."

Slipping on hugely popular gore, they flee the scene.

"I am Simon Bestwick and this is Maddie Finnegan."

The hunchback performs a mock curtsy and offers a greasy handshake. They have reached the unofficial market area, packed with covered wagons full of instrument makers and conductors.

"I suppose you want my name in exchange? It's Tim Rice. Perhaps you have heard of me? I used to be a lyricist for musical plays. It all went wrong when my partner turned pretentious. We were doing fine, giving the audience stuff bordering on the pop sensibilities of the Hippy Era. Then he got weird ideas about cultural status. We've been enemies ever since. It's odd how we've both ended up here, trapped in Hell with only one way out. In our minds, you see, this horror."

"And what is that supposed to mean?"

"I'm weary of talking. I want a slobbery pastime."

Maddie lifts her hands and grimaces as Tim throws an arm around her waist and puckers his decaying lips for a kiss. "Get off me, you leprous librettist! You boil in the bag buffoon!"

Simon comes to her aid. "You prosaic paddy-field!"

Tim relaxes his attentions and shrugs sardonically. "You can't deny I was handsome once. You'll be like me soon. It gets to you, these small increments in misfortune. Devils in the sewers, unnatural storms, rivers of gore, carnivorous statues, sentient tridents, reality holes — I don't think the scars ever heal. The flesh gives up, stops regenerating itself in the old way. Life was garbed in finery up there. Down here, it's been stripped and molested, but permitted to shield its modesty with a single garment — a technicolour nightmare coat!"

"Tell us more about Green David and the juke-box."

Tim coughs and wipes globules of lung from his chin. "He wasn't bad in the beginning, but he travelled around India on a bus. Who knows what he picked up spiritually as well as deep in the gut? He opened that pub, the Hell's Bells, to collect mortals for his amusement. Fools regard his thatched trap as a slice of heritage. I'm glad he took my colleague, but I'm innocent. He's a monster, a pervert."

"And what is the nature of his perversion?"

"Nothing to be treated with much sympathy. There are numerous views as to how he earned his name. Some say his flesh is coated with luminous slime, others that he dines solely on emeralds and celery. I can't vouch for either rumour, but I think he was a jazz musician who chanced on the perfect melody, the most haunting tune ever written. You know how catchy jingles stay in the brain, go round and round and refuse to depart? They dominate the conscious mind, pushing other mentations aside. Now imagine the effect a perfect jingle would have on listeners. It would completely swamp their thoughts, omitting all else."

Simon is sceptical. "And that's what Green David composed? Then why isn't he famous? I haven't heard of him."

"He kept his melody secret. He recorded a private version of it for his juke-box. How could he go public with his skin condition? Don't know how his bar staff abide it, or remain immune to the tune. Besides, if he released the record, civilisation would grind to a halt. It's impossible to hear it and continue normal life. The listener falls into themselves, becomes catatonic, at one with the song."

Maddie tugs at her earrings. "I get it. But wouldn't a perfect tune envelop the planet in ineffable ecstasy?"

"Yes, if played in a major key. Green David transposed the piece by a semitone, turning it into the most perfect miserable melody. Listeners are sucked into an infernal empathy — an acoustic Hell. We're sitting in the pub at this instant, but we think we're here. It's a total mirage, a saturation of our intellects with music."

"Explain how an escape might be organised."

"When Green David finished the song he added an extra note right at the beginning, a gratuitous crotchet which disrupted the ensuing series. With the extra note, the melody was no longer perfect. It could be heard without pulling a listener into an inner Hell. That's how the rascal was able to record it safely. Then he sabotaged his antique juke-box so that the needle of the pick-up jumps this first note. Everybody who goes into the pub and selects his number hears the perfect version. By duplicating the missing note we can return to Earth."

"Simple. Only twelve semitones in a scale."

"It's not just the pitch of a note but its timbre, its tone-colour, attack and decay, its precise signal. Not all notes are sine-waves, most are far richer, with complex harmonics. To get free from Hell we have to calculate the exact qualities of the original crotchet. That's why we're all studying music theory. Green David, beneath the layers of his anger, has a sense of sportsmanship. He's fitted Hell with composing materials, journals on acoustics, newspapers with concert reviews, metronomes, inks and blank staves — in short everything an enterprising sinner might need to score the actual note and perform it."

"What instrument was used in the original?"

"We all disagree on that point. The more I think about it, the more I am convinced Green David built his own fretted contraption with unique characteristics. Plucked like a mandolin, but it might have been a chest of teeth strung with jugular veins. Didn't you notice a squelchy cadence to the chorus? I don't suppose you did. The point is, everyone has their own bleary memory of the desired crotchet. Only by stealing each other's work can we arrive at a true picture of what it was really like. With my latest prize I've finally collected enough notes to estimate the average sound. My euphonious ticket out of here!"

"Why not simply share your information? Then everybody can leave in one go. Why all this fighting and blood?"

"You suppose my colleague wants me back up top? If he escapes first he'll smash the juke-box, leaving me trapped inside the melody. No, it's every celebrity for himself. He spies on me day and night, not that such terms are relevant here. When I obtain a new manuscript he seems to know what it is. That's why I've got to keep this one secret and open it in a secluded place. My shack is quite close."

Tim is interrupted by a wild shout from the centre of the market. A globe rises over the wagons, hissing. It is a balloon of pompous design, huge canopy secured by orange netting to a wooden crate. Simon points at this abomination and swallows his horror.

"What's happening over there? Should we run away?"

"It's Branson. He thinks he can escape from Hell by air. His eighth attempt. Spent months eating beans to generate the required methane, the imbecile! Green David can't be swindled."

Slowly the balloon lifts into the sky, dropping coprolitic ballast. A bellow of encouragement drifts after them. Maddie notes two figures in the basket, both flashing carious smiles. The canopy bounces against the ceiling and one of the circular hatches set in the rock swings open with a sombre clang. Something square emerges.

It is a brass bedstead, complete with knobs and stained mattress. A mannequin dressed as a Swiss nun, parasol in one hand, reins controlling the apparatus in the other, sits propped against the pillows. The pilots of the balloon release gas in a desperate attempt to land. Swooping down towards them, the bedstead makes a showy loop, rattling and warping from the tensity of such somnolent aerobatics.

The mannequin puts aside its parasol, gropes under a pillow. Now it has a gun in its fist, a bizarre automatic pistol with a stock made from bunched twigs. Simon, who is a minor expert on historical firearms, lets loose a howl of astonishment and respect.

"A Besom-Handled Mauser!"

Uranium bullets strike the balloon. The explosion is less turbulent than Maddie and Simon expect, but it illuminates the duskiest corners of the market. Strips of burning fabric snake through the smoky air. With a monumental tinkle the crate lands on a procession of baby tridents which are winding their way between dustbins and stalls. The wooden sides fall apart to disclose passengers like kebabs.

Simon is nauseated. He watches as the bedstead dives on a stall and the mannequin catches bundles of documents from the owner with the crook of its parasol. It repeats the action eight times, returning through the circular door, which slams shut behind it. "So many brown-paper packages tied up with string! Why sequester them?"

Tim laughs briefly. "Good job it didn't get mine. They are a few of its favourite things. Come on, let's go to my shack. My colleague is out there, I can feel his putrid eyes on me."

They climb painfully up a hill by the side of an art gallery which lures victims with the odour of formaldehyde and inches of bare flesh glimpsed through cracks in the wall. The hill is cobbled with knuckles and Tim is close to collapse on the ascent, damaged lungs rasping like pork bellows in a mosque. Simon is becoming delirious, he knows that one more hour in Hell will finish him, turn him into one of the grim folk. He prays to an unspecified god that Tim is no charlatan.

Halfway up the path, growing at an unlikely angle, a mound of earth and bench betray the presence of a Municipal Persontrap. The umbrella is new, stone stalk thrashing as they pass. There is a corresponding cavity in the sky in which huddles a ruby cloud.

The summit of the hill is only five feet below the roof. Maddie has to stoop to avoid striking her head, Tim is already hunched at the right angle, Simon has few problems. The shack in question is made from sheets of asbestos cemented together with bile. Next to it storm-drains gargle. At the rear of the shack stands a peculiar machine, a musical instrument of chaotic design, entwined with tubes and hung with bladders, bells and bottles. Dustbin lids rock on spikes, lengths of wire coil in loops over drumskins, triangles and xylophone slats.

Tim rotates the bundle in his hands.

"Aren't you going to read it?" Simon enquires.

"Not in the open. It's too important to take such a risk. I need to crouch under Maddie's skirt for privacy."

She shakes a fist. "Don't you dare, or I'll pummel your ganglia. No versifier is allowed beneath my hemline."

"Be rational, it's for the sake of our souls."

Considering this, Maddie eventually nods assent. "Alright, but just Tim. Well hurry up and get it over with."

"Stand still." He wriggles under the skirt. "It's too dark, anybody got a light?" Simon gropes in his pocket for a box of matches, pushes it to Tim. There is a scrape of phosphor on sandpaper, the sound of tearing envelope. Maddie makes a sour face as moans of satisfaction emerge. Then the mutant is back in the fresh air, clapping his palms, his foul visage crinkled in a mirth more conducive to ugliness than his earlier anxiety. He showers mutilated flaps of manuscript.

"I've got it! Now we can be out of here in fifteen minutes. First I must adjust the tuning of my Riceophone."

Easing himself into the shack, he fiddles with his machine, peeling gilt off bells, tightening or slackening wires, oiling valves with sweat and licking pedals. Finally he fills the array of bottles with a noxious liquid from his dangling member, tapping their necks to check the pitch. Maddie and Simon lurk impatiently during this delicate operation, unable to repress a gruff cheer when he is done.

"Hold this cymbal steady and I'll set the machine going. Powered by clockwork it is, rather like the demons."

"And the rumpus it makes will return us home?"

"That is correct, trust me. The missing note."

As they move forward, a humourless laugh from behind persuades them to spin in alarm. They are confronted by an apparition in an opera cloak and absurd hairstyle, mouth full of eyes.

"He's lying, he always lies to newcomers. False poet!"

Simon clenches his fists. "You're the man who offered to exchange a textbook of music for our handkerchiefs."

The figure bows gracefully. "And now I'm the fellow who thinks it's best to rip away the comforting veil draping your vision. You are naught but unpromoted pawns! I'm the genius, all others are fools. I brought in urgent revenue, I invigorated the scene."

Tim whimpers. "It's my colleague. Don't listen to anything he says. He's the liar, not me!" Pouncing on his rival, he throws unhygienic arms around his neck. "Leave us, Lloyd Webber! I've worked hard to be free of your influence. So hard! Let me go back."

"Sorry, it just isn't proper. Rice must never be served on its own. You're staying put, special fried Timmy."

"Andrew, we loved each other once. Please release me."

"Acting catty, am I? Well don't cry for me, Basmati, the truth is I never left you. All through my dark days, my bland existence, I broke my promise, don't keep your distance. Squatting beneath Maddie's thighs was a masterstroke — literally. But I have equipped the sewers with a system of mirrors. I'm able to monitor every district of Hades at a glance. She stood above a storm-drain and I saw all."

Maddie steps in to separate the adversaries. "What's all this fuss? Let's return to Petersfield as a team..."

"Told you that was possible, did he? But Green David's arranged for only one to escape. After that the extra note's useless. It'll fade away like any other echo. We think the same, him and I. His mind is almost as profound as my own. I guessed there'd be enough mirrors down here for my scheme. Wardrobes get damned too, you know. So I sat back and waited for Timmy to do the work. Now I'm ready to steal his victory. I have no love for silly old England, only good for staging my shows. But I long to see Ireland again, with its lower tax rates."

Maddie glowers at them both. "If it's true that only one can return from Hell, we're not interested. We'll find another way out. Simon and I intend to stick together, come what may."

Simon nods slowly. "Loyalty and justice. Moral stuff."

"That's your mistake, elf-chops. Now stand back and let me through. I'm wasting time talking to untermensch."

Tim shudders, grumbles and falls away. He wants to oppose his enemy but his self-esteem is too low. He weeps.

As the man in the opera cloak approaches the shack, a horrid gurgle follows him. He looks over his shoulder to admonish Tim but the lyricist has a sealed mouth. Someone else is climbing the hill, on all fours, mad words dribbling from bloated lips, scraps of paper speared on long nose, eyes flickering like drowning glow-worms. His speed is astonishing, much too fast for a sane metabolism. Already his spleen is overheating, black smoke spiralling from holes in his shirt.

Tim shouts a warning. "It's Barry! His mind's snapped. Three demons came out from a manhole and destroyed his work. He doesn't need a stick, he gathers manuscripts on his proboscis."

The man in the opera cloak is also concerned. "If he maintains this trajectory he'll collide with the shack."

"The Riceophone must be protected. Someone assist us!"

Maddie utters a thin laugh. She is ready to leave, but Simon's hand reaches for his belt, unbuckles it, draws it through his loops and gives it to Tim. His trousers fall down. "Trip the crooner up with this!" Both celebrities grip opposite ends of the leather strap. It is Maddie's turn to feel left out, while the men solve the problem. Barry is rapidly upon them, accelerating. Tim and Andrew look rather good as a team, stringing the belt across the track, collaborating.

The impact knocks them sprawling. They wriggle across each other as Simon weaves the belt around their limbs.

"Help me, we'll truss them up good."

Despite his modest stature, Simon's strength is not inconsiderable. With Maddie's aid, the three professional entertainers are soon bound in a compact orb. Securing the buckle, the newcomers rest awhile, listening to the cajolements of the slimy notables.

"Give it a kick," Simon says. "You know where to aim."

A pugnacious look crosses Maddie's face. Her boot connects with the circumference of the flesh ball. Down the hill it bounces, straight into the province of the Municipal Persontrap.

The stone parasol bends and opens to receive the gift. The flexible cap shuts firmly and the whole sculpture shakes violently. Muffled cries from within are quickly replaced by acute screams. The shaking lasts for many minutes, the cacophony gradually diminishing. At last the cap spits out gristle, molars and a salad of indigestible items — nose, hairstyle, member, a cheekful of feminine blue eyes.

"That's wrapped things up quite well." Maddie turns to congratulate her companion but he is gone. He is hurrying to the shack, tripping over his trousers in his haste to save himself. "You turncoat!" she blusters. He reaches the instrument, locates a handle and winds the device with an apologetic shrug. Maddie does not follow.

"Sorry, girl. Remain here if you insist, but I'm off."

The handle will go no further. Simon releases it and fumbles for an ignition button. There is a lever by the side of the row of bottles. For a moment it seems jammed. He leans against it with his entire weight and its shifts into gear. Somewhere a spring gives up its frustration. Right at the heart of the machine, cogs rotate.

"It's happening, Maddie! I'll drink to your memory. Here comes that emancipating note. My freedom is sorted."

Mallets slide into position, automated batons tap. The whole device shakes on its foundation. Then it speaks.

A A A O O O Z O R A Z A Z Z Z A I E O Z A Z A E E E I
I I Z A I E O Z O A K H O E O O O Y T H O E Z A O Z !

Simon opens his mouth to shout in glee. There is a pause, his tears are unsalted, like those shed at a nut's wake.

"It didn't work! I'm still here. What was that noise?"

Maddie's answer is soft. "The sound of music in Hell."

"So what's the right note?"

She bends over to pick up Tim's sharpened stick. She leans on it as she climbs to the shack. Simon is standing in his underpants. Flimsy and paisley they offer no protection. He pretends not to notice as she lifts the stake for a single, ineluctable blow.

His scream is very unusual.

Maddie squints at her surroundings. A bar with a brass rail, tall stools and low tables, dartboard, juke-box. She is back in the pub. The pointed stick is still in her hand, with a piece of Simon dangling from the end. Apart from a barmaid, the building seems to be empty. Peering closer she sees this member of staff is a mannequin dressed as a Swiss nun. Why had she not noticed it before? Probably because Simon bought the drinks. But in that case, why had he said nothing?

It is of no consequence now. She is safe and alone. She stumbles to the front door, then turns with a frown. Where does Green David keep his other victims? She decides to try the cellar. The access hatch resembles one of the rusty portals in the ceiling of

Hell. Her tormentor obviously has specific tastes. She descends a ladder into nigritude. The blackness is not complete. As her eyes refocus she beholds a massive chamber lined with rows of stiff grimacing cadavers.

Most are ordinary humans, travellers who stopped for a drink in the town. Others are recognisable as public personalities. She strolls among them, prodding a selection almost scornfully — Elton John, Damien Hirst, Barry Manilow, Andrew Lloyd Webber, Per Lindstrand. In the sixth row she locates Simon, his trousers puddled around his ankles, his manhood sadly lacking. She feels a sudden sympathy for him and returns the part with a shake of her stick. It adheres easily.

A shaft of green light strikes the corpse next to him. Something is shuffling closer from the back of the cellar. Without caring to discover its exact nature, Maddie clambers up the ladder, scurries out of the pub and closes the door behind her. In the hot sun of Petersfield, the music shops and curry houses appear encrusted with verdigris. The spectrum has been spoiled for her. Lacking envy, she mounts her motorbike and belches off into the mercifully blue distance.

Ribbons

Simon Bestwick

Ribbons sits in the living room, licking blood from his fingers. He picks up the baby's arm and tosses it up into the air, trying to catch the end with the hand. He gets the soggy end once or twice which is unusual for him; his coordination is usually spot-on. On this occasion, however, he is somewhat tired. He's killed nearly a dozen people today, after all.

Bored with the game after a while, he gets up and wanders through the house. The October sky is dropping into dusk outside the window, streetlamps like hot embers nailed to banks of lowering cloud. Night turns rows of houses into jagged silhouettes like broken battlements.

He steps over the father's body, which lies by the foot of the stairs, head at an angle because his neck is little more than a rag, mostly blown away by the silenced glaser slug. He walks up the bathroom and pisses, then into the parent's room. He toys with the mother's underthings, sniffing the crotch of a pair of lacy black knickers. No odour but that of Lenor.

He reminds himself to check the linen bin in the bathroom for used knickers. But the kid's bedroom is calling, and he follows it.

The baby's cot is as he left it, the infant's severed head jammed onto one of its posts, gazing at him incuriously with the dead blue marbles of its eyes. He wonders if there are any marbles in the house, that he can substitute for the eyes before he leaves.

The mother lies on her side against the cot legs. Her neck too is broken, but by a blow rather than by a bullet. He wanted her unmarked. The skin of her throat didn't even have time to bruise before she died. He was merciful. No he wasn't. The reasons were aesthetic, not altruistic.

He rolls her onto her back and rips off her blouse, then her skirt and knickers, which he throws aside. He drags her stiffening legs apart and unfastens his trousers, then penetrates her.

Her naked body is cold to the touch. It is the coldness that excites him. The heat of living bodies makes him uncomfortable. It reminds him of friends' blood- back when he had friends, before he dismissed the whole concept- splattered over him, and of the heat bred by decay in piles of the rotting dead, as it soon will in her and the others.

He fondles her cold breasts and kisses her death-slack mouth. She is perfect now. There is always this moment in between death and decay. Cool perfection. The beauty of a timeless statue.

He ejaculates, then withdraws and pushes his penis into her prised open mouth, thrusting in and out till he is hard. She is like a sex doll, but infinitely more erotic to him.

When he has achieved erection once more, he turns her over and pushes his penis into her anus. He grips and paws her as he ruts, then comes again.

Finished, he pulls away in a spasm of self-disgust. Not with the act itself, but with the motions it excites. He hears his grunts, like a pig. Fortunately there is a stereo in the room. He turns it on to drown out the remembered noise. He wipes at his face with clawing, dragging motions to remove the sheath of sweat she's pulled out of him, horribly hot.

Angry at her for making him an animal, enraged at the coarseness she has provoked, he draws the automatic and shoots her again and again, with angry method, destroying first her breasts, then her crotch and buttocks. He pumps rounds into her midriff to complete the destruction. When he has finished, the torso has been completely destroyed. Only her arms, legs and head remain. He dangles one off each corner of the bed, finally propping her head on the pillows, her hair braided deftly into ponytails tied with red, red ribbons.

There is a chair by the window. He sits here and opens a crack for the light breeze. He loves October nights. Led Zeppelin is playing on the stereo. No Quarter. He likes it, the soft bubbling synth, rising, the high cracked croon of the vocal, soft as the menace of wind-chimes on a Hallowe'en night.

Green and the others found the first bodies around eight o'clock, the first of three families killed by McCauley. The father had been crucified on the kitchen wall. One child, a seven year old girl, hung upside down from the hall light, gutted, stomach cavity opened out like wings, a red ribbon- the calling card- tied round her throat. The other child was a five year old boy. His head was propped on the newel post of the stairs. His skull had been hollowed and his eyes gouged out. A candle's light flickered through the empty sockets like a pumpkin lantern. Early for Hallowe'en, Green thought but did not say.

The mother was in the upstairs bedroom. He probably fucked her after he killed her, but the body was so badly mutilated and dismembered that Green doubted they'd ever find out for sure. He knew, though. He knew the nature of this beast.

"How long?" he asked.

"Couple of hours." Franklin, their medic, said.

"He won't have gone far. He's hot now. Spread out. North, south, east and west-" may god's holy name be blessed, he thought but again did not say, an old snatch of rhymed prayer from schooldays. "Track him. If you get the scent, shout."

They nodded.

Ribbons listens to No Quarter till the last minute or so. The bass stays constant but the voices grow out of tune and discordant. Intentionally too, it seems, which he can never understand. Why ruin a good tune like that? Piqued, he pumps a round into the stereo, and watches flames dance among the wreckage. One of his knives has an insulated handle and he slices the cord with it. Later he watches the fires sputter and die under a towel.

He wanders downstairs and makes a cup of coffee, searching through cupboards and fridge for food while the kettle boils. He finds bacon and white bread, and switches on the grill.

While the food cooks, he sits at the kitchen table and sips his coffee, placing his gun on the table beside him. They won't take much longer to come, he know that. He sighs.

He prefers to use the knives in his knapsack. They come in all shapes and sizes, little stilettos and throwing blades, through army-surplus survival knives to nine-inch butcher knives and machetes. He loves using them, the sense of power. Any fool can use a gun, but it takes talent to use a knife well. Knives don't just kill, they transform. They shape. Like whittling a figure from wood. As he shapes these into new shapes. What would they have done with their lives anyway? Now they make something else, artwork, transient but beautiful like ice sculpture. That was art, its bravery, its beauty, its defiant shout in face of entropy and decay. The art fades and crumbles but we persevere, shaping new and more awesome works to flower briefly before forgetfulness rolls over them.

Almost absently, he picks up a knife and plays with it, tossing it spinning up into the air and catching it again, far more fluently than the baby's arm, then weaving patterns with its sparkling metal in the air. He was always good with knives. That was why they called him Ribbons. His little trademark, the little length of red silk that decorated the bodies like a painter's signature, had grown out of that, not the other way round. But, the gun has its uses, such as when you're in a hurry. Or if the wrong people come bursting through the door.

He eats his sandwich and smokes a cigarette. After a while he starts to sing Show Me The Way To Go Home.

*

Green entered the second house.

There were more of them this time. The daughter was a teenager, and had two friends round. The mother had had a friend round too. The father sat against the wall in the hall. His skull had been split open and his genitals hacked off and jammed into the gap. Clearly McCauley had considered him a dickhead.

The mother and friend's breasts had been cut off and hung from the lamp in the centre of the ceiling, stitched up to resemble balloons. A red ribbon was tied around the stem of the lamp in a gaudy bow.

Upstairs had, apparently, been the scene of an orgy, albeit necrophiliac in nature. 'Apparently' because McCauley's disgust at the heat engendered in him had overspilled into frenzy. The walls and floor looked like a Jackson Pollock painting. The fragments were jammed into the corner of the room; it was impossible to tell one piece from another.

One of Green's men ran to the bathroom and vomited. He came back shamefaced and pale. Green patted him on the shoulder. "Don't worry about it. First time isn't it?"

The lad nodded; he didn't trust himself to speak.

"I was the same on mine. Buy you a drink later. Got a fix on him yet?"

"Sir," responded Jackson, another veteran. "Couple of streets away. He seems to be staying put."

"Probably waiting for us. Lock and load, lads. Just in case."

Ribbons makes another cup of coffee and continues to wait.

He thinks about Angela, his girlfriend. He met her a couple of months after he left the Army and moved in with her not long after. She'd been young, small, tanned from a summer in Spain, and eager. Very eager. Hot and eager. So hot.

She tried. It didn't work. Nothing helped. The feel of her hot little body only made him remember Falkland Sound. Remember the dead and the time he was trapped with his dead comrades. There was little heat where they were but enough for them to rot. Only the added warmth of their decay had kept him alive.

He liked Angela, he maybe even loved her. But the feel of her, lying with her, however hard she tried, brought it all back. Handcuffing her to the bed didn't work. Or beating her. Even raping her was no good. Nothing could overcome the warmth. He wept over the bruises he gave her, but still that didn't heal them. She cringed from his touch, afraid to let him, but at length would accept it, even more afraid not to.

He kept her locked in the flat while he toured the sex shops to bring things back to try. One time he caught her trying to climb out of the window. He beat her, then raped her on the spur of the moment. It still didn't work. He started drugging her after that, making her drink coffee laced with tranquillisers and waiting till she was asleep before he left. One time he came back and she was still asleep. He tried it then, when she was silent and still and he could pretend she was a doll. Dolls didn't work, but this combination was somehow better. If she only wasn't so damned warm. Warmth. Heat. Rot. Dirt. Decay. Death.

Death.

It was then that he hit on the answer. He pondered and mulled and agonised for some time while she lay sleeping. She wouldn't feel a thing. She loved him. She'd said so. She wanted to make him happy. This would. But she might chicken out if it came to the crunch, and he couldn't have borne that. Best not to ask. Remember her saying she'd do anything for him. Take her at her word and keep the best, avoid the worst.

The slender red ribbon was beautiful and he contemplated it for a long time before wrapping it round her throat. Rather than discolour her sweet face- the last batch of bruises had almost healed- he used it as leverage to snap her neck. He could have done it bare-handed, but this seemed somehow more right. She didn't feel a thing. Sleep became death in an eyeblink.

He lay by her and stroked and fondled her. She was still too warm. He had to be careful and get her at just the right time, when she was cool but before she could stiffen.

He lay there naked by her as the shadows deepened to night. He turned on the light. Her tan was fading. After another hour she was cool enough. He got on top of her and began.

He kept going all night. She was never satisfied, never too tired to go again. He explored every orifice from every angle, used many of the toys he'd bought and had fun, but in the end, it was best between just the two of them with no fripperies to get in the way. She was perfect at last.

Rigor mortis had come of course, but it doesn't last forever. As it onset he experimented with positions, getting her into just the right one to keep things interesting and open to possibilities for the twelve or so hours it should last. He rested after a while of it and positioned her on all fours. He sat near the bed and watched her as he smoked. He lit another cigarette and popped it in her open mouth, anchoring it in a corner, and placing an ashtray underneath as he watched it burn down. He took it from her lips before it could burn right down and scorch the flesh.

The best moment, he thought later, came as the rigor wore off and she began to slump down, her upper body first, arse up in the air, then the rest of her. When she was limp once more, they began again.

Things went well for the next couple of days. He'd turned the heating off to prolong it as far as possible, but in the end Angela had started to get warm again. He cried when he realised it wasn't just his imagination or his own imparted body heat. She'd let him down. He started hitting her, fascinated by her bruiseless skin, but stopping when his fists made dents he couldn't straighten out.

He fucked her one last time, a wild rout of desperation, and that was when he'd seen himself from the outside, a flash of realisation. A naked, grunting hog. An animal. She'd made him like that, shameful, a rutting thing, disgusting, sweating from the heat. His heat. No. Hers. The heat she'd made him give off.

He got his knives out then and began to chop and hack and slice, redecorating the room with her, and taking a fresh pleasure in this last partnership. She helped him. Helped him become more than a beast again. She'd taken his humanity but gave it back now.

It was then, when he stood in the dripping cavern of the room, among the ruins of her body, that he knew his destiny. He'd left that day, and set off looking for his next lover.

They caught him in the end, but that's part of the game. He's loose again now. This latest round of lovers has been typically suburban, orgies and quickies behind closed doors. Next time, just one, maybe two, and make it last a couple of days. Sweet and tender. He's been without for a while now, and it had made him greedy. Next time he'll pace himself.

At that point the front door blows in, as does the back. A gun is pressed to his neck. He doesn't reach for his own, but smiles and stubs his cigarette out as Green and his men swamp the kitchen. The right people have found him.

They took McCauley out to the van, while Green called for a clean-up squad for the third time that night. The young man who'd thrown up drove Green back, following the van to the Facility. Neither spoke.

When McCauley was settled back in his quarters, Green went to see him.

McCauley sat at his desk, playing his song- Ribbons by the Sisters Of Mercy. A hard, jagged bass and acoustic, narrowing down to a sharp point, the vocal trembling on the edge of hysteria all the time, spurting occasionally into it before the shutters slammed down again.

"You took some finding that time."

"With all that technology?"

"Power lines and shit. They interfere with the transmitter."

"I'll bear that in mind."

"That took some clearing up. I hope you're not planning on making a habit of this."

"Don't worry. I was desperate for it. Any idea how long it's been? I'll tell you, too long. But, no-" McCauley stretched luxuriantly. "-next time I'll go for something more like a romantic weekend, you know. You can't beat it."

"I'm sure. Well, now for the bad news. Leave's over. You've got a job, first thing Monday."

"Big?"

"Why else would they send for you?"

"Good point. Tell me tomorrow. I'm tired right now."

"OK."

Green closed the spyhole and stood in front of the door for a while. He always felt nervous after talking to McCauley, watched somehow. The guy gave him the creeps. They might need him to do the dirty work- he was the most efficient killer Green had ever heard of- but he didn't have to like it. Then again, wasn't that what duty was all about?

Green turned and walked down the corridor.

And in his cell, Ribbons McCauley smiled his secret smile and wound a red, red ribbon through his fingers and over his knuckles, loops and cat's cradles, like the paths and waterfalls of an intricate stream of blood.

Brass Monkeys
Jason Davison

Herbert sat, patiently waiting. Watching the hours tick by, sometimes dreaming of the best reactions, but mostly just waiting. The excitement increasing as time drew nearer. He'd heard the weather report last night, frosty with snow later. This made his mind up, a shiver of delight jumping up his spine just to think of being out in the snow again. The first fall of the year was special, he couldn't miss this for anything. First thing in the morning, before light even, he rang work, fobbing them off with a story about how his mother had fallen down the stairs and he'd had to take her hospital.

'Time enough' he thought finally seeing the first flakes. He got up and went to get changed into his personally tailored winter suit. It was without exception the single most important creation in his life. This one set of garments gave his whole other wise banal life meaning. From it he gained excitement, danger, adventure and relief all in one fowl swoop. He paid meticulous attention to the creases in his trousers. It had to run parallel to the vertical line of the musty green chequered pattern, which almost without noticing blended perfectly with the brown and faint orange squares.

Finally dressed he stood in front of a huge brass edged mirror, proud, rehearsing his new adjustments to the show. It was a simple, elegant few steps, loosely (very loosely) based on the phantom of the opera he'd seen earlier in the year. His haunting beauty. Yet was it his distorted view of himself through the mirror, or did the steps look uncomfortable, slotting together with an untidy jerking motion. It must be the heat he thought to himself. When the chosen audience viewed it they'd see the seamless elegance of the steps, secretly admiring his subtle interpretation. Out there in the whitened town all the sharp ugliness of modern life was now sheened over, giving it a rounded, more sculptured refinement. The same went for Herbert's show, that's why it had to be out in the snow.

After placing on his peaked cap (green and black chequered), he told one final look at himself in the mirror. Smiled at himself, then headed for the door buttoning up his long coat as he did.

"Mother" Herbert shouted "Mother, I'm going for a stroll down the park. Shan't be to long". There wasn't any answer, but he didn't expect there to be. Why should he? She had lost her hearing six years ago. Old age, don't you know.

By the time he arrived at the park gates there was an evenly pasted lair of snow blanketing everything, a few faint footprints impregnating it. The number of people out had also dwindled considerably. He slowly walked along a row of neatly shaped conifer's, which obscured the wall of a building behind. This was the side of a café which stretched from the front gate of the park, some fifty yards along to where there was a risen level, slabbed and scattered with plastic patio sets. Next to this were five aviaries pushed together just that little bit to snugly, huddling together for warmth like a group of their occupants, a couple of snowy owls with their yearlings snuggling together for warmth. Towards the far end of the aviaries were various islands of bushes surrounded by thin channels of tarmac and grass, all dyed white. This was to be his hunting ground. 'Plenty of cover for this years show' he thought. Now all he had to do was to watch and wait. The best place was in the Carillon tower where he could take in most of the park in one go. But first he needed a warm drink, and one to take away.

Four hours past by as he stood there gargoyle like on the second floor of the carillon, his head peering between the pillars on the second floor. The green had totally vanished now except for sparse showings on each tree. The horizontal of a hat and coat of the first person to bear the weather in half an hour. The paths now thin compressed tracks of snow. 'Finally someone who looks worthy of the show.' The perfect candidate, a feminine looking woman for the time of year, walking alone.

His semi-numbed body immediately warmed with excitement. He watched as she strolled, shoulders hunched, straight towards his designated stage, which was obscured on all sides by bushes. By the looks of it there would be no one able to interrupt him for several minutes. That would be plenty of time. He quickly rushed down the staircase and back out into the snow. Covering the three hundred feet to the 'stage' his blood swelling in his throbbing body. He could barely contain the excitement. Then he slowed to a snail's pace just before he reached the corner of the bushes, shivering with excitement; quickly unbuttoning his long coat, while keeping the illusion of it being closed by leaving the top button fastened.

There she was; his next choice. The accidentally lucky viewer, she was just thirty or forty feet away. 'Smoothly does it' he told himself under his breath. As he walked nearer and nearer he could see that they would converge just after the park bench. Then he replaced his eyes to the ground. As he reached the metal bench he saw her feet trenching towards him. He slowly lifted his head to make eye contact before revealing his crotchless trousers and everything else. He opened his coat as he smiled at her. She started to smile back and then as he revealed himself her expression changed. First to shock as her mouth dropped open, then to anger, her brow and top of nose crunching up. She started yelling at him then smacked him bang in the face twisting his whole body as he fell. He landed with a thud, head first on the back rest of the bench, knocking him out cold.

He woke, head throbbing, sprawled out over the park bench. Looking up he saw a bleared image of the woman in the distance pointing to him and talking to a man in black. Realising that the man was of the police his senses quickly came to, and he yanked himself from the bench to make a hasty get away.

But by doing this he'd without realising ripped the lower part of his glued ball sack off the frozen metal bench, leaving behind his testicles in a pool of raspberry slush. He grabbed at the blooded heap and headed off in the opposite direction crouched forwards in agony. His one hand holding his balls, the other holdin what was still left

A Thin Disguise
Christian Saunders

It had been just another day for Marcus Lewis, nine tedious and stressful hours trapped in a stuffy office sorting out other peoples petty financial problems. And all the while with his pretentious prick of a boss breathing down his neck. throwing deadline after deadline at him, pressurising him, increasing his workload daily.

And this was quite possibly Marcus' most despised part of the day; The endless crawl home across town in rush hour traffic, his back aching, eyelids drooping and head pounding, thumping, swirling. Full to bursting point with numbers. He felt tired and used.

Momentarily he had a waking vision, his weary head finally admitting defeat and actually exploding, spraying a vile mixture of blood, tissue and fleshy brain matter all over the train compartment and his startled fellow commuters. In addition to the gore, there were numbers everywhere - sickly, obscene, throbbing numbers dancing in the air to an unheard tune. Blood soaked and festering.

Marcus's eyes snapped open and he shook his head violently from side to side. Couldn't fall asleep, not yet. The soothing rhythmic clattering of the train seemed to be hypnotising him, making it increasingly difficult to keep his eyes open, never mind focus them. His head was swimming. Oh, how he longed to be safely home so he could take off this soffocating mask and strip himself of the thin disguise that enveloped him.

It was almost dark when Marcus finally inserted the key into his front door. By now he was sweating profously, simultaneously panting and quivering with excitement. It seemed like a lifetime since he was last home - warm, safe and secure. The door swung inward, welcoming him.

Once inside, he stood completely motionless for a few minutes, breathing heavily and savouring the moment. Then he slowly peeled off his overcoat, removed his tie, then his shoes. gradually, the speed of his actions increased until a primal, almost sexual urge took him. He hastily clawed at his shirt, ripping off a button in the process but not noticing, and not caring if he did. His trousers followed, then his socks, nylon vest and finally his soiled underpants.

Only then did he start fumbling blindly for the light switch on the wall. The finale to his strange and ritualistic striptease was the careful removal of his gold watch, st. Christopher and chunky signet ring which he wore to the office - for Marcus, this signified the stripping of the last remaining trinkets linking him to his other (daytime) life. The jewellry was placed on a small, practical looking oak coffee table.

The ritual was carried out in an eerie silence as Marcus possessed no television, VCR or hi-fi (useless non-essential electronic rubbish). Then he made his way to the bathroom where he showered for over an hour, rubbing furiously at himself with soap, sponges and flanels. When at last he was satisfied that no lingering trace of dirt or grime contaminated his slick, naked body, he dabbed himself dry with the fluffiest of towels and made his way casually to the bedroom, his favourite place, humming softly and admiring himself at every opportunity along the way.

Marcus sat at his dressing table, studying himself in detail in the glorious huge mirror. He ran his fingers over the velvet smooth skin of his chest and carressed his pert nipples, sighing with satisfaction. Suddenly his eyes widened in terror. STUBBLE ! It couldn't be. No, not stubble. Relieved, he realised that a single hair protruded cheekily from his skin, just beneath the left nipple. He plucked it between his thumb and forefinger, wincing even though he actually liked the delicate stab of pain and the resulting warm tingle.

Marcus was very fussy about his chest. And his arms. And his legs. In fact, he absolutely detested body hair of all kinds, especially that tangled and messy clump down below, forever seeking to obscure his most favourable feature. That was why he spent literally hours every week systematically shaving and plucking every square inch of his body.

Except, of course, the unkempt ginger growth which covered his throat and lower face. Although shaving had become a compulsion, Marcus loved his beard. It was a feeble last line of defence against the outside world, offering at least partial protection. Another barrier to hide behind.

Marcus opened a drawer in the dressing table and took out his make-up set. With a certain amount of anguish (nothing seemed to match his eye colour - an exquisite dark shade of brown) he selected the necessary nail varnish, lipstick, eye shadow and mascara. Then he applied them, skillfully and with a sense of purpose of which any proffessional would be proud. He was guided in his work by the hand of experience.

While he did it, Marcus continued to hum softly and let his mind wander. All thoughts of numbers had thankfully departed. Instead, he thought long and hard about madness. He thought about this quite a lot. It is said that a true madman is not aware of his condition as the thin line between fiction and reality becomes increasingly blurred. He knew that his actions were not those of any normal person and so decided a long time ago that he was not insane, for the simple fact that if he was, he wouldn't know. He was just different, thats' all.

In the worst possible scenario, he saw life as a single, infinitely long path winding its way gracefully through a dark, dense forest. Occasionally, he would leave the well - travelled path and venture, of his own accord, into the surrounding black wilderness where he would stumble around blindly for a few hours exploring, before locating (admittedly, he sometimes had difficulty doing this) and rejoining the path. He knew it was risky but was full of admiration for his own strength and courage. And besides, if he didn't explore then he definately would lose his marbles. As any news report suggested, being part of the stifling rat race had already proved too much for alot of people. Release was the key.

Marcus wished, above all else, that society would allow individuals to be individual. He was sick and tired of being bound by unseen social restraints, each and every day growing tighter until they left you used and suffocated, a shadow of your true self. But deep down he knew that his dream would never be allowed to come to fruition, the anonymous powers that be would never permit it. Modern people were all far too concerned with public image, and how their's could suffer. One day Marcus would show them all the right way to live by going to work without his disguise. That would get the tongues wagging wouldn't it? Who knows, maybe some of the more courageus mites caught up in the rat race would follow his example. He would be a hero!

Now it was high time for a spot of pure self indulgence. Marcus opened a second drawer in the dressing table and took out his sewing kit, one of his favourite items.

Selecting an especially long, sharp needle, he proceeded to pierce his ivory white left thigh. Once, twice, three times - each thrust slightly harder than the last, driving the point ever deeper into the flesh. Blood trickled down his baby - smooth leg and onto his twitching foot. He smiled and moaned in ecstasy, feeling so alive, so liberated, so in-control.

However, all too soon, enough was enough. Still stark naked (believing clothes to be little more than useless fashion accessories) Marcus got up. He felt weak and groggy and his makeup was in danger of being completely ruined by his watering eyes. He made his way unsteadily back to the bathroom where he showered once more, gently rinsing away the congealing blood and patchy, smeard makeup. Cleanliness was important to him.

When, at last he had finished, he made a mockery of his daily routine by going back to the dressing table. It was late, he should get to bed, but the mere thought of having to once more don his fake exterior in the morning was simply too much to handle. He cocked his head to one side and stared at himself in the mirror, soon becoming lost in his bottomless, dark eyes.

His wounded leg had started to bleed again, but Marcus was oblivious. Now would be the perfect time to make his stand, to reveal himself to the world. He had been in hiding for far too long, it just wasn't healthy.

Marcus had suddenly, inexplicably, came to a conclusion. Never again shall he fear the ridicule or snide remarks of his peers, for it was just as much his world as it was theirs. How did they know that it was he who was strange, it could well be that they were abnormal, not least for continuously suppressing their desires and ignoring their true vocation in life. It was wrong that he should be hidden away within these four bare walls.

Quivering with excitement and anticipation, he went to bed with Leon, his special friend.

The next morning, Marcus was awake bright and early. It was to be a big day for him and he felt suitably refreshed, invigorated even. So much so that he spent over two hours before the mirror, carefully applying layer after layer of bright, garish makeup. Of course, he couldn't resist the odd stab with his precious needle. Perhaps he over did it slightly.

Then it was time to go to work. As this was a red - letter day, Marcus called a taxi. He stood silently at the door waiting for that impatient bleep of the car horn with blood oozing from a hundred tiny wounds scattered all over his body. The needle itself protruded from his bloody naval like a flag pole.

He felt faint and occasionally had to lean against the wall to avoid collapsing in a heap, smearing it with a sticky maroon pattern. He was frightened and aprehensive, but he knew he must be strong. He must set an example.

Anyway, he had his long beard for protection, and in one hand as a precautionary measure, Leon the gore-streaked teddy bear dangled. In the other clenched fist he held an eight-inch stainless steel carving knife for any interfering shit who gave him a hard time. Or even so much as a funny look.

Suck And Blow

Jane Fell

The vacuum cleaner hulked, skulking in the dark cobwebbed corner - of mind: throwing down a challenge, (do some work for once, you slut) - sounded like it was talking to her, sounded like her mother' s voice swearing and cursing her, calling her a lazy fucking bitch.

The cluttered room begging to be dusted, and vacuumed and rearranged. Didn't know where to start. So she didn't. No interest in the house that was no home - (her own fault). She felt just like part of the shabby furniture, faded and uncomfortable.

No good, she would have to make some token effort to mend, or at least tidy what threatened to become a broken home. She stopped picking the hard skin (more dust), off her dirty feet and got up off the settee. Did a bit of dry dusting (no polish) unprofessionally. Just passed a rag back and forward across the wood - just scattering the dust around. Unsettled - she waited for the voice to sound again; but it didn't.

She approached the vacuum, unwound the tangled flex that was split in places, dangerously, coloured veins exposed. She'd have to start vacuuming the cobwebs in the corner: she could not find the attachment for the carpet. Cleaner plugged in, but not yet switched on: started on her anyway. Having it seemed, a mind and a life of its own (more than she had).

Its huge, thick, springy rubber (safe sex) penis snaking around and between her legs. The hose winding upwards, tightly - touching her hot crotch. She giggled uneasily to please. A little thing like a pair of scanty panties not getting in its way - thrusting and ramming right up her cunt. No screaming; breath knocked out of her as it had her off her feet, the heavy cylinder on top of her - dust bag leaking - on her chest making her cough, when given leeway to breathe, to gasp.

Hose rammed up through her intestines mangling, spleen (venting) rupturing, and bladder bursting. Foul smell of pissing and shitting self. Ribs splintered - lungs punctured full of blood. The snake rocketing out of her mouth (a bleeding heart in it) as she vomited, heaved up her innards, spewing guts. Thrown all round attached to the cleaner, shaking crushing her. It disemboweled her, all internal organs messily damaged, beyond hope - repair - foul stench of despair in thick diminishing air. Her pulped head bursting out of her arse (talking through it) - one word (help!) garbled (with blood) bubbled, like in a comic strip (her clothes tangled and slippery with her torn entrails) - thinking aloud; reading aloud. Slow learner.

An old story - a strange, cruel twist; her head and neck pulled in (wanted to hide) and wrenched through her already torn and brutalised vagina. Reborn: wanted her mummy. Mummy dead. A vacuum left. Perishing in her sex - turning on self whining at the daughter (pull yourself together). Reborn, sucked - wet mess of faeces and blood and piss - dry. Half-dead: and half-alive (on her father' s side); but death a formality - in the bag.

She woke trying to scream, hearing the vacuum still keening: she was chewing her pillow stifling her screaming - broke free, and wailed with the sound of the cleaner. Her poor mum dead: at last. And what had her ever loving daughter ever done for her?

Did it on behalf of her mother, who had always been so house-proud. Had dropped the urn on the carpet, contents spilling out, and vacuumed them up - ashes to dust. Had done it while drunk. Staggered over to the vacuum, now, and put it on blow. Brains, guts and gore splattered up the walls. The house, so grudgingly cleaned for the wake, a bloody mess again. Her mum was bleeding right - swore her daughter was frigging useless., And would be till her dying day having hers.

That's What You Get For Being A Smart Arse

Darren Floyd

Frankie was cracked. The crack snaked from his abdomen across his scrawny chest, branched up his gnarled neck, and split his face in two. His hair looked as though he'd just received a shock: despite his best efforts with gel and furious brushing, it still stood in black spiked exclamation marks. Most people couldn't see the crack, but many suspected it was there. Certainly the Sergeant and Brian thought he was cracked. Perhaps it was the way he seemed possessed when someone put "You're Gorgeous" on the Juke Box. He stood behind the bar at the Madienlake shouting the lyrics accusingly.

"Because YOU'RE gorgeous! I'd DO anything for YOU!"

He made the song sound like a threat, with his eyes lolling around in his head, like two marbles in a gold fish bowl. The regulars in the Madienlake would look at him uneasily. At his day job in the slaughterhouse his work mates would break into a sweat when he sliced through animal carcass with obvious enjoyment and zeal. Frankie was cracked. This was just an every day fact of life, until the day The Dishwasher arrived.

Fiona had been going out with Frankie for three months, which was two and three-quarter months too long for her. They'd got together after a drunken fumble at her cousin's engagement party. To this day she didn't know why Frankie had been there, and more importantly she couldn't understand why she was still with him. She sat with him on the sofa in her flat. Tonight she was going to tell him that it was all over. For the moment, though, Frankie was having a regular rant about Michael "Mikey" Parish, the landlord of the Madienlake.

"I hate the way he looks down his nose at me, throwing his weight around. Mind you, he's got enough weight to throw with his big fat gut!" Frankie laughed at his own 'witticism'. Fiona's face creased in a strained smile.

"He acts the big 'I am' around the place." But that's because he is the big 'I am', thought Fiona. She watched Frankie with a growing feeling of helplessness, knowing that she wasn't going to get a word in edge ways. She sat back on the sofa, and thought about her little secret, her savings account that she was adding to week by week. Money that was going to buy her a one way ticket to Australia, and a new life. She allowed herself a smile and daydreamed about her escape.

"I do all the hard work while Mikey slowly gets fuck-faced with the regulars." Frankie fumed.

"So why don't you leave?" asked Fiona

The reason for that, thought Frankie, is because I have my hand in the till and I'm robbing Mikey blind.

"I need the money", mumbled Frankie in reply. At the end of the night Frankie had wound himself up so much that all he was in the mood for was a quick kiss and a half hearted grope, much to Fiona's relief.

It wasn't actually just the landlord that Frankie hated. He hated most of the regulars as well. In particular, thought Frankie, I hate that pair of old spunkers Brian and the Sergeant. Frankie stood behind the bar of the Madienlake and looked at them coolly, as they sat playing draughts in their corner. They're probably moaning about me now, he thought.

The Sergeant turned back to the game of draughts.

"That bloody clown Frankie thinks that we haven't got anything better to do than gossip about him."

Brian made a derisive snort. Their corner smelled of damp and was stained yellow with the smoke from Brian's Woodbines.

The Sergeant considered his move, and continued to speak.

"I remember having an argument with him about British Beef. Just because the little shit works in a slaughterhouse he thinks he knows it all!" The Sergeant made a move, and instantly congratulated himself; get out of that one, you thick bastard, he thought as he watched Brian consider the board. You really are a sorry excuse for a man, five foot nothing with those few hairs combed over your egg head, and I bet you regret having "Gene Vincent" tattooed on your neck. The Sergeant realised that he was staring at Brian, looked back at the board and carried on with his story.

"I thought he was going to hit me for a moment in that argument. It's lucky for him that he didn't. I may not be a Spring

Chicken anymore, but the army training is still there you know." The Sergeant said making practice karate swipes with his hands.

Army training my cock, thought Brian, rolling another Woodbine. You never made it past Private, you bullshitting bastard, but you've let everyone forget that. Sergeant by Christ! Have this, you smart arse.

Brian moved one of his pieces. The Sergeant frowned.

"Yeah, I remember his first night here." said Brian dismissively .

"He only gave me the wrong glass! And then moaned like a bloody woman!" Brian put on a whinging voice, which wasn't far removed from his own.

"It's my first night, he said, I don't know what glass it is! Well, I told him, didn't Mikey train you properly? It's a jug with a Kangaroo Keyring on the handle. It's kept beneath the crisps. He only gave me Paul's bloody glass! So I told him, mine's got a yellow Kangaroo Keyring on the handle. What a twat!"

Brian sipped the pint of Dark Mild that Frankie had spat in, like virtually ever pint he'd ever poured for Brian. He put his pint down and won the game.

"Another game?" Brian suggested smugly

"No." The Sergeant said, annoyed. They sat in their corner, watching the traffic go by, and wondered what to do with the rest of the day.

Since Tracey the barmaid had left (Mikey didn't know why she'd left, but suspected that it was down to that piece of shit

Frankie), it was taking longer and longer to clean up at night. Some glasses weren't getting as clean as they should, and- what was worse- on some occasions he'd had to help out himself. So after a request had been put into the Brewery he'd been given the cash to buy a Dishwasher. Now, he could have gone to the Cash and Carry and just bought one. But Mikey had a mate, Gary, who could sort him out with a perfectly functional Dishwasher at half the price, plus all the required receipts for the Brewery and the Taxman. Lovely.

Except for Frankie it was far from lovely because the Dishwasher hated him. He could tell that Mikey had got it cheap. It was a large bulky thing, resplendent in white plastic and chrome, it was made by a company called "Hampton Co", Frankie had never heard of them. It had three chunky lights, green, amber, and red. When red flashed up it was supposed to show that the Washer had finished. Frankie had read, and re-read the manual "Welcome to the Hampton 2000! The End of the Most Odious of Domestic Chores!" But the machine didn't seem to work the same way twice. The red button flashed, Frankie opened it up and pulled out a tray of glasses, only to have the machine start up again and spit scalding water out at him.

"Fucking machine!" Frankie shouted giving it a kick, it promptly gave him a shock.

"Oi! Mikey that cheap piece of shit you've bought just gave me a shock. It's a fucking hazard!"

But Mikey was laughing too hard to reply. And so it was, another thorn in Frankie's already prickly side. He became involved in an ongoing battle of wits with The Dishwasher. Then one night it got worse. The Dishwasher began to speak to him.

That night, Frankie's head felt like a volcano about to explode. Nothing had gone right all day. He'd felt wound up almost as soon as he'd woken. Frankie thought that hacking and slashing at the slaughterhouse would help with the frustration, but he'd got a bit too carried away. He'd made a clumsy cut into a prime carcass. His supervisor had seen this and ripped a shred off him, and worse still told him that the price of the meat would get docked from his wages! Frankie had started to complain, but then had been threatened with the sack. He'd gone back to work with the whole episode replaying in his head, and he began to hack and slash again.

Then he was sitting in an opulently furnished room. Around him well dressed men with slick backed hair sat smoking, reading broad sheet newspapers, and drinking tea. He watched as a waiter left a silver pot of tea, nodded at him and went about his business. He tried to get up, without success, and realised that he was a spectator to the unfolding events.

A man walked up to the table and greeted him with a polite but formal "Good afternoon." Instinctively he knew the man's name was Timothy Williams-Jones, and he was visiting him today in the role of ambassador.

Williams-Jones was dressed smart but casual, with a brown sweater and cream flannel trousers, his blond hair was brylcreemed back, and a neatly trimmed moustache underlined his nose.

"I see that little upstart is still making noise in Germany." Williams-Jones said gesturing to the front page of the paper on his table.

"Yes, but I'm sure Neville will teach him a lesson." he heard himself say *"You haven't come here to discuss world politics with me."*

"Indeed. It's well known that for the past few years that you've been studying the Black Arts, that recently you gone beyond the theoretical, and that in the past few months you have began to practice them."

"Practice? I can assure you that there has been nothing tentative in what I've been doing recently."

"What ever." Williams-Jones said impatiently. *"You are not the only one who has been pr...studying the occult. Lord Warren Joyce is considered to be a Master in The Forbidden Arts. He has heard that you have been rather...disparaging about his skills."*

"I was led to understand that his Magick skills, or rather lack of them was a matter of fact, which I was just confirming. I am by far his superior." He heard himself say nonchalantly as he picked an imaginary piece of twine from his sleeve.

Williams-Jones looked furious, but he managed to bite back his anger.

"Lord Joyce demands satisfaction! He invites you to settle this like Gentlemen!"

"Certainly, we shall meet after Supper at Lumley's Club in Mayfair on Tuesday. There I'll teach the illegitimate Irish prick a lesson." This last bit he heard himself say while stifling a yawn.

Williams-Jones face drained of colour,and without further comment he briskly turned on his heels and marched out of the tea room.

Frankie felt the sides of his mouth crease in a smug grin, he went back to reading his paper then-

a wet sixteen year old work experience grunt was in the wrong place, at the wrong time. Frankie sliced clean through the grunt's hand. Frankie looked around bewildered, now back in the familiar surroundings of the slaughterhouse. The grunt's hand landed on a conveyer belt and trundled away with the rest of the scrag ends of meat and offal that would eventually end up in Cornish Pasties. The grunt squealed like a pig while he clutched the stump where his hand had been seconds earlier. Frankie couldn't stop laughing as the blood splattered his face, people rushed to the grunts help. After the blood had settled Frankie was sacked.

So now Frankie had to be on his best behaviour at the Madienlake, because until he could find something else, he had to live off the wages from the pub. He spent the evening biting his tongue and swallowing the blood. He was still trying to make sense of his vision. Frankie remembered hearing someone say that even if you tried the Mushrooms just once you could still get flashbacks years later, but was that it? Had it just been a flashback?

It was the end of the night, and he was cleaning up alone. Mikey had gone to bed (lazy bastard). He had been replacing a bottle of Glenfiddich Malt Whisky when it had slipped out of his scarred, scabby hand, and smashed. Frankie looked down flabbergasted as the amber liquid spread across the floor, there was no way this he could hide the missing bottle. As sure as shit Mikey would dock it from his wages. FUCK! FUCK! FUCK! He started kicking the bar. His foot connected with a shelf of fruit juice bottles. A sleet of juice and glass rained across the bar. A shard of glass ripped across Frankie's check, the blood splattered across the Dishwasher, and quickly disappeared. Frankie didn't feel the cut, he just continued to kick, and kick until there were no bottles left. He slumped against the bar to catch his breath ; Christ, he felt so tired ...

...and then he was looking out at an unfamiliar, dimly lit room. There was the smell of burning spices and incense. He was aware of a circle of people watching him intently. As the vision solidified around him he also became aware of sweat dripping off his face and body. He felt as though he'd run a marathon. He felt so tired. Across from him sat a man in the lotus position. He was well dressed, but it looked as though he'd just had a heavy night. The man's hair was plastered to his head, his jacket was open, his bow tie was undone, and his piercing green eyes were blood shot and had bags under them. He realised that this man had to be Lord Warren Joyce from his previous vision. A chalk circle surrounded both of them. The air was heavy with anticipation.Somehow, he knew that he'd been locked in a battle with the man across from him for some time, and both of them were considering their next and final move. He felt his concentration lapse for a split second, but that's all Warren-Joyce needed. He smirked, brought his hands together, and threw them wide apart, muttering something in a

language that he didn't recognise, but thought that he should. He felt himself being ripped from his body. He heard himself shout something that left Warren-Joyce looking shocked. Then-

"Do you feel better now?" whispered a refined voice.

Frankie jumped a mile.

"Who the fuck is that?"

Frankie picked up one of the smashed bottles by the neck and held it in-front of him like a knife. He wasn't able to guess where the voice had come from, he suspiciously scanned the dark bar. He heard a sigh.

"I showed you what happened, and what you see before are the consequences."

Frankie looked at the Dishwasher and was instantly aware that the voice in his head came from it.

"We battled for forty hours! The invisible dimensions were torn asunder! Incantations last whispered by The Ancients were *roared* into the ether!"

"And you lost," interrupted Frankie, with a lop-sided grin.

"It was a draw," stated the Dishwasher with a note of menace. "Lord Joyce was well aware of my distaste for menial tasks. He tore my soul away like a mussel from its shell. He originally imprisoned me in a machine the size of this bar. I was pressed into service at the Hilton. Over the years as successive machines have worn out I have been transferred to different machines, until I find myself here." The disgust was evident in his voice. "Joyce had no sense of flair or imagination, he caught me with a cheap little Irish hex. Condemned to the never ending life of a washer woman! I only wish I could have seen the effects that my last magick spell had upon him."

"So if this pub's not good enough for you, why come awake now little Lord Fuck Face?"

The Dishwasher ignored Frankie's insult, but answered his question.

"Because, *boy*, I have never encountered a psyche as cracked as yours before! It was me who squirmed into the gaps in your mind, and gave you the visions. I've been guiding you. Your blood was a catalyst. I can feel my shackles weaken. You and I will make a formidable team."

"Oh yeah, I can see it now," snorted Frankie. "Us going down the pub together. I'll have a pint of lager, and a bottle of Fairy Liquid for my pal the Dishwasher here! Fuck off!"

"For all your energy, you're not overloaded with brains, are you boy? You are the key to unlock the door of my prison."

Frankie cocked his head, and looked sceptical.

"What's in it for me?"

"Vengeance." dripped the Dishwasher.

Tonight's the night, thought Fiona. She couldn't bottle out now anyway even if she wanted to, she'd booked her plane tickets. Come Monday, she'd be leaving this shit tip behind for a new life.

Frankie persuaded her to come back to the Madienlake for a little after hours drink. Fiona was nervous: she could never remember the Madienlake having a lock in, and he seemed a little *too* keen to get her there. He'd unlocked the door, and disappeared inside. Fiona had reluctantly followed him. She'd expected to see the usual suspects in the bar, but instead it was deserted, and all the lights were out. Frankie was nowhere to be seen. She started to get worried.

"Frankie?" she called as Frankie brought a fire extinguisher down on her head. Fiona fell unconscious to the floor.

He dragged her around to the bar, and stuffed her head in the dishwasher. Frankie was damp with sweat, but the voice in his head had told him that he was doing well. He'd had to break her legs to fit the whole body in to the machine. Fiona's screams were drowned out by the whirl of the hungry machine as it boiled her face. He eased the Dishwasher door open slightly and sneaked a look inside, Frankie felt himself grow hard looking at the carnage. When the machine had finished he retrieved what remained of Fiona and hid her in the cellar. When he came back Frankie leaned on the bar and opened a bottle of Newcastle Brown.

"That was fun. What now?" asked Frankie.

The machine moaned and sighed a contented "More."

Mikey Parish looked out at the bar and wondered how much longer he'd have a job. Since Penny his wife had walked out he'd tried to cope, but had given up caring months ago. The brewery was already breathing down his neck. His thoughts were cut short when the pub's internal phone rang. It was Frankie calling from the Cellar. Mikey listened getting increasingly annoyed at the prospect of having to sort out Franke's incompetence, again.

"Look, it should be fine. You should be able to sort it out, I shouldn't have to come down." Said Mikey.

"Well, if you paid a full time cellar man you wouldn't have to come down." replied Frankie.

He's for the high jump, sarky bastard, thought Mikey.

"Okay. I'll be down now." He put the phone down, and turned to the Sergeant.

"It's that bloody Frankie. He's got his thumb that far up his arse he needs me to come down and pull it out for him."

The Sergeant chuckled as Mikey left the bar to help Frankie. It was the last time anyone saw the landlord of the Madienlake alive. Mikey slowly descended the stairs, he opened the cellar door to inky darkness. He flicked the light switch to no effect.

"What are you playing at?" were the last words Michael "Mikey" Parish ever said as a beer cask came crashing down on his skull. Frankie pulled the body to a corner of the cellar. He began to work with the knives and mincing machine he'd 'borrowed' from the slaughterhouse.

Tired, but happy, Frankie emerged from the cellar.

"About bloody time too. Have you changed your clothes?" asked Brian.

"Yeah, well, you know the mess beer can make." Brian didn't recognise the look in Frankie's eyes; he actually looked pleased to be behind the bar, and happy to be serving. This put Brian in a better than usual mood. He took a sip from the pint that Frankie had just poured for him.

"That's really nice, it's uh, really…." Brian fumbled for the right phrase.

"Full bodied?" offered Frankie.

"Yeah, you took the words right out of my mouth."

Frankie grinned.

Frankie was in the cellar, stripped to the waist, and standing in a chalk circle. Strange symbols were drawn into the cold stone floor, similar signs were daubed across Frankie's chest in blood. A circle of candles around the chalk circle illuminated the cellar. At Frankie's feet were the remains of Mikey and Fiona.

"What now?"

"Just say after me…" Slowly Frankie repeated the words the voice whispered in his head. The flames from the candles grew higher and higher until they formed a ring of fire. The lifeless bodies of Fiona and Mikey got up slowly as if pulled by an invisible string. They linked arms around Frankie and slowly began to turn. Upstairs in the bar, the dishwasher began to bubble and melt, until a pool of metal lay burning the lino floor. It slinkied down the cellar stairs. The metal pooled at the cellar door and stopped as if in surprise at the strange dance in front of it. Suddenly it sprang into the air like a jack-in-the-box, and joined the dance, forming an orbiting ring around the corpses and Frankie. The liquid metal ring constricted, tendrils branched out and snaked up Frankie's nostrils, poured into his mouth burning the back of his throat. Finally it wound itself around his thigh, and snaked up his sphincter.

"You queer bent bastard." Frankie muttered, but felt himself get erect. The river of metal branched into his ears, gouged troughs through his skin, and drained into every available orifice. His back arched, and he gave a pleasured moan. Metal soaked into his bones, muscles popped and were plated with chrome, his skin rippled and grew tough. He felt cold fingers curl around his spinal column, and a presence liquefy into his brain. He stretched and heard bones crack. The molten metal should have burned and scarred his fresh, instead it had left a series of crimson canals over his body. For the first time in his life the voices in his head were a perfect sweet symphony of hate.

Instinctively he knew what needed to be done next. He bucked and heaved, vomit sprang from his mouth and seeped into the beer barrels. His back straightened and finally his erection came to fruition, his sperm rained into the barrels. He broke a bottle and made a slit in his palm, blood joined the rest of his fluids into the barrels. When he'd finished he got dressed, smiled and left.

It was opening time at the Madienlake. Frankie drew back the bolts of the front door, and the usual seven people walked in, led by Brian and the Sergeant.

The Sergeant looked vaguely worried as he looked at Frankie. He seemed somehow taller, and there were strange scars over him.

"Those haven't anything to do with the abattoir have they?" he asked Frankie, nervously gesturing at the ridges.

"You know women, ha, ha!" Frankie chuckled in response. The Sergeant didn't quite know what he was getting at, but felt compelled to laugh along anyway. Frankie's voice seemed deeper, and if the Sergeant didn't know better he'd say that it seemed to have an echo on it as well. Frankie looked at the regulars intently with a sparkle in his eyes. Brian held his pint up to the light.

"Is this the first one off the barrel?"Brian complained, "It looks cloudy."

"New barrel? Nah. If it tastes off, I'll not only give you a free pint, but I'll also give you your money back.Now you can't say fairer than that can you?"

"Suppose not." mumbled Brian and drank. He took the pint from his lips.

"It's not often I say this, but that's..." he started coughing and couldn't get the rest of his words out. Brian's coughs seemed contagious, the coughs spread in a Mexican wave around the rest of the regulars in the bar. Glasses smashed as they fell out of the hands of the convulsing customers. The Sergeant's head whipped wildly around as the effects of the pint took hold. The skin on Brian's face began to blister and burn, white liquid poured from his mouth and his eyes. Cracks issued across their burning skin. Seven pairs of dead eyes looked out at the bar. But they weren't eyes; sunk deep into the zombies flesh were red bulbs like the ones that had once been part of the Dishwasher.

Frankie leaped over the bar and gave his newly metallised body a stretch. The magician was now part part of Frankie, and through his eyes they both looked at their motley zombie army. It wasn't much, but it was a start.

Frankie opened the bar door and looked out . Followed by the newly zombified regulars Frankie stepped into a sunny new day.

Damaged Goods

Julia Jones

"I'll ring Watchdog."

"But you can go back and get another can of beans."

"I don't want another can of beans, I want those beans. Those beans are the only ones my babbies will eat."

"I...uh...I..."

"Give them to me for free."

"I can't..."

"What else are you going to do with them, their damaged goods, but I'll have them. They are the only ones my babbies will eat."

"I'll have to call my supervisor."

Cathy could feel anger and shame boiling inside her.

The woman with the beans crossed her arms across her chest, rolled her eyes, and sighed. The sigh echoed down the cue behind her like a line of falling dominoes, joined by the occasional tut.

The dim lighting exaggerated the lines and bags on everyone's faces, and made them look ill. The place stank of pine disinfectant

When Diane the supervisor arrived she instantly let the woman have the beans for free. The women clutched her beans as though it was the Holy Grail, while her lips formed into a cruel smile of triumph.

"You didn't need me to do that." Diane whispered into Cathy's ear. "Do it yourself next time."

The next person in the cue began to put her food though, Cathy couldn't look her in the face.

Cathy tried not to think about what her supervisor had said, but it reverberated. The sky on her walk home was concrete grey. A few times Cathy thought that there was someone behind her, running at her just about to hit, she'd turn around but there was no one there. She cut through the industrial estate on her way home. The wind rustled disturbing the rubbish that had collected in the drains. The curb was smeared with dog shit. The scars on her wrists and arms began to ache as it began to rain.

Some kids hung around a vandalised phone box; broken glass lay in water filled potholes. Cathy looked down at her feet as she walked past the kids; she heard them sniggering and calling her names as she passed.

She opened her front door, her forehead furrowed with crease.

Do it yourself next time. Yeah, how could she be so stupid, she wished she could go back in time and do things differently. It had been one of her good days, but now it had turned to bad. She knew that her evening would be spoiled worrying about what would happen in work tomorrow.

"Alright love, I've done us Pizza and chips." Colin said as she got in. The house smelled of fried food.

Cathy didn't answer, walking straight up stairs to change; she didn't look in the mirror on the way up.

Dressed in a pair of leggings and sweatshirt, her hair tied back she came down stairs.

Colin could see that something was wrong as soon as he saw her, his spirits sunk.

"What's wrong." He tried hard to stop himself being annoyed.

"There's nothing wrong." She mumbled.

"I can see something's wrong, you've got a face like a slapped arse, what…"

"I said there's *nothing fucking wrong, stop bugging me!* Alright?" she yelled pushing past him.

Colin clenched his teeth and fists.

"I was just…"

"I don't care…" she sat down in front of the TV with her Pizza and chips. Cathy stared at the food.

"I'm sorry…it's just…something happened in work…it just upset me…"

"But that's not my fault."

"I know it's not *your fault.* I never said it was *your fault.* I was just telling you…"

"You know what the Doctor said about winding yourself up…"

"I know, I know, it's just you know, sometimes things just…get on top of me."

"Are you having your period?"

She dug her fingernails into her palm until it bled.

Cathy lay awake as Colin snored. She could still see the Artex on the ceiling. Except for the snores all was quite, she could hear was the sound of an occasional boy racer revving his car up the street.

Cath's eyes were wide open, and in the silence the voices began.

She lay in the bath looking at the mildew and the peeling wallpaper. She's managed to avoid Colin and his constant questioning to see if she was "All right." Cathy knew that he was doing it because he cared, but part of her thought that he was only doing it because that's what people did on the TV. He didn't really want to know how she was. He didn't really care. He just didn't want to seem like a bastard.

Her orange peel thighs lay in the water, the water turning their colour fish skin.

"Look at you, you disgusting blob." The voices said. "You disgusting fat pig, you fucking disgusting mountain of lard."

Cathy raked her well-bitten fingernails down her thighs, the cellulite disappearing under white furrows. She did it again and again until she cut into the skin. She started to pull the flesh out turning the bath water red. Exhausted she climbed out unsteadily; Cathy soaked up the blood running down her legs with a grimy towel, and bandaged them up the best she could. She got dressed to go to work.

Although it was still cold the weather had brightened up since the previous night. Cathy thought she could smell the beginnings of spring. A tentative smile creased her face at the thought of warmer times. She hadn't always been like this, when Cathy had been a kid she'd been really bright, there had even been whispers of college, but somehow that had all slipped. Now here she was in a cut-price life she'd never wanted.

The sound of a laughing little girl playing with a dog drew her attention. She looked across the road. The girl wasn't playing with the dog she was kicking it, hard. Every time she did it the dog would whimper, but then drag itself back to the girl who would give it more abuse.

Cathy felt a scolding anger burn inside her. She ground her teeth until she developed a headache. The voices started to talk. Cathy looked down at the cracks in the concrete and tried to ignore them, but one phrase kept coming back to her:

"This is all your life is, and it's all your life will ever be." Shut up, shut up, shut up.

"Shut up!" she yelled. Some school kids pointed at her and laughed.

Although Cathy tried to hide it, all the customers she served mentioned her mood. Diane looked over and at her and frowned.

"You're going to get sacked! You're going to get sacked! You stupid cunt. You stupid fat cow you're going to get the sack from a simple check out job."

Cathy dropped a bottle of Toilet Duck she was putting through the bar code reader.

"Stop it!" she screamed.

The customer jumped back from the till.

"What did you say to me?" the customer said with an air of disgust in her voice.

"I wasn't talking to you." Cathy spat.

"Who were you talking to then?"

"I…" She looked down at the dirt ingrained in the tiles on the floor.

Diane ran over to Cathy.

"Go on your break now, I'll replace you."

"I don't know what…I should…I don't…" Cathy said starting to sob. She was fumbled out of her seat and ran to the staff room.

In the room she stared blankley across at the sink. A chipped yellow Formica table was in front of her, with a foil tray, which once had been home to a Bakewell Tart, but was now overflowing with cigarette butts. Also on the table was a dog eared copy of Heat magazine. The cover had pictures of Jennifer Aniston and Brad Pitt, and Victoria and David Beckham, "Shopping Secrets of the Stars!" Cathy opened the magazine and stared at the stars and their shopping, picture after picture of them going into exclusive shops,

Cathy couldn't work out why they'd been printed, and couldn't work out why she couldn't stop looking at them.

She turned a page to see Kylie Minogue at an awards ceremony.

"Have you seen my new mobile?" Cathy could overhear to girls talking.

"Gives us a look…that's lush!"

"I got a good deal on it, and I've got the ringtone on it from Pop Idols."

"Lush! I going to get one of those next pay day."

"Oh don't talk I have to pay for my holiday. Two weeks in Spain."

"Lovely!"

Cathy put the magazine down as the voices started.

"That's all their lives revolve around insignificant details. When people ring on their mobiles they have nothing to say to nobodies with trivial lives. They work all year round for two weeks of regimented *freedom* with the rest of the herd. And these two shallow nothings have more in their lives than you."

Cathy cradled her head in her arms

"What is happening to me? I don't know what's happening to me?" she muttered.

"Can I have a word in my office." Cathy looked up to see Diane. She followed her past the two girls who were now talking about the Survivor TV show.

Cathy only heard fragments of what Diane was saying.

"...have been excellent...model worker...chance at promotion...last few months...unreliable...been given chances...sickness...sickness...sickness...what's wrong with you? Cathy, what's wrong with you?"

She focussed when the question was asked again. Cathy thought for a moment, then decided to tell the truth.

"I don't know. I don't know what's happening to me, it's like someone is burying me alive. The more I struggle to get up the more muck people throw on me, I can feel myself getting covered and there's like nothing I can do about it, I'm going further down into the blackness, and the voices..."

Diane's eyebrows arched in concern.

"The what?"

Cathy looked down and mumbled: "Nothing."

Diane took a deep breath.

"We're going to have let you go, I'm sorry..."

"Let go? Let go, what do you mean? *Say what you mean!*" Cathy screamed spit flying onto Diane's desk.

"You're sacked get out."

Cathy screamed again, she was still screaming when the security guards threw her out.

"You've done it now."

"Shut up."

"People are looking, people are looking at you you embarrassing fat cow."

"Shut up."

"Can't even keep a simple cashier job you stupid cunt."

"Shut up shit up shut up shut up shut up!" she screamed. Cathy flailed and spun, her vision becoming mixed up and confused like interference on a TV set. She looked around desperately for sanctuary. Seeing a public toilet she stumbled towards it.

The toilet was dark, cold, and smelled of human waste. Three quarters of a mirror remained attached to the wall; someone had spray painted "Bastards" in red over it. Cathy looked at her reflection; she looked like a dog.

From the closed toilet cubicle behind her came the sound of a wino's guttural mumbling, every once and awhile the word "Nothing." become audible.

Cathy turned the taps on and a splutter of cold water came out, she splashed it on her face. It didn't help.

"Mmmmm, bhastards, therrllll paaaayyyyy the bhastards....nothing."

The mumbling was becoming louder.

"What can I do?" Cathy whispered.

"Nothing." said the wino.

"Shut up."

Then the voice from behind the toilet door became clear and crisp. It was not a voice she'd ever heard before.

"Nothing you will do will make a difference, you are sailing towards the darkness. In thirty years no one will remember you ever existed. In sixty years no one you knew will be alive. It wouldn't matter if you'd never lived. This is the best you get. After life there is nothing but darkness"

Cathy's eyes grew wide with horror as the voice spoke. She looked again at her reflection in the mirror and saw the seeds of her own ageing and death, and knew that the voice was right. Cathy clawed at her face, trying to erase what she saw. Her fingernails dug into the skin and shredded it, sending tears of blood down her face.

The voice started to talk again, but Cathy didn't want to hear anymore, she ran out screaming and tearing at her face.

"I don't know we, well I, had talked about a kid, maybe if we'd had a kid…" Colin's voice trailed off.

The Doctor nodded, and peaked at his watch while Colin wasn't looking.

"Will she…"

"It's hard to say." The Doctor said cutting Colin off. "Given her past history this was always on the cards, but the severity is extreme. She is very heavily sedated, and she will have to remain so for the foreseeable future."

"Right, well, I uh, I've got to go…"

"You can go in and visit her if you want." prompted the Doctor.

"No, I've got to go, you know stuff to do…get the car sorted."

"I understand." The Doctor opened the door and Colin left without looking back.

A string of saliva hung from Cathy's lips as she sat slumped in a chair, surrounded by patients who were as equally as vacant as her. There were no more voices, there was no more anything. She stared out catatonically at Who Wants To Be A Millionaire.

Poor Things

Gary Greenwood

A crow sat on a barbed wire fence and pecked at a sheep's eye. The sheep moaned mournfully, twitching as it tried to free itself from the crow's beak and the tangled mess of wires it had run into during the night. Something had tried to take a bite from its hind quarters at some point, but the sheep had still had the strength to lash out then. The blood stained wool, however, beckoned to any scavengers that happened to pass. The sheep could feel their gaze upon it even as its own was torn from its socket.

"It is a poor thing to eat while one's food still lives,"

The crow started, the eyeball hanging from his beak, twirling as if it too looked for the speaker.

A hare sat a few feet away, ears turning and twisting, its fur blending in with the overgrown weeds and grasses, the uncared for vegetation bleached brown by the long summer. They stared at each other for a moment before the crow flicked his head, catapulting the sheep's eye into the air. With elegant ease, he tilted his head back, beak wide open, and swallowed the orb as it dropped into his mouth. Below him, the sheep groaned again as if in protest and pain.

The crow turned to the hare.

"It is a poorer thing to starve when food is before you,"

They stared at each other a while longer, the crow swaying on the wire slightly, a combination of the wind and the sheep's dying struggles. The hare's ears twitched constantly until, with an irritated grunt, he gave in and scratched at his head with his hind foot. The crow chuckled at the hare's discomfort and flapped from the swinging wire to the nearest wooden post.

"What brings you to this field?" the crow asked the hare.

"Curiosity, mostly," the hare said, shrugging his shoulders. "I'd heard that all the men have gone,"

The crow laughed again. "The men haven't gone," he said, watching as the hare instantly lost his relaxed stance, becoming the watchful, nervous creature his kind were. The crow narrowed his dark eyes, staring at the hare. "They haven't gone. They're dead."

"What?" the hare whispered after the crow's words had sunk in.

"They're all dead, hare. Everywhere I've been there's dead men. Not one left standing."

The hare stood up on his back legs, looking around as if he half-expected to see a field of men, flat on their backs or standing limp like the farmer's scarecrow. At the thought, he turned back to the crow and asked if the farmer, too, was dead.

"He was a man, wasn't he?" The hare nodded. "Then he's dead. He's down in his house, flyblown and bloated, him and his wife." The crow's eyes sparkled as an idea came to him. "You want to come and see?"

The hare hesitated. "I'm not sure. How far is it?"

"The way I fly? A couple of minutes,"

"How long will it take me?"

"I don't know," the crow said. "I've never had to run anywhere." He laughed again, looking down at the sheep in the wire. At some point in the conversation it had died, its remaining eye glazing over, looking nowhere near as appetising as its counterpart had.

"What's your name?" he asked the hare as he raised his head.

"Mizieya," the hare replied. "What's yours?"

"You know the way to the farmhouse?" the crow asked, ignoring his question. "Straight on through this fence, down the next field and hang a left at the potato plants. You'll come to a bramble hedge; go along that until you come to an abandoned tractor. There's an open gate nearby that'll take you out into the lane. Follow that down the hill and you'll come to the house."

With a flap of his wings, the crow launched himself from the wooden post and into the air.

Mizieya stared at the limp body of the sheep for a while before hopping over to the fence. Avoiding the body, he quickly dug a shallow dip beneath the wire and squeezed under. He glanced back at the sheep for only a second before running out into the field.

The crow circled above him until he was sure he was on his way, then soared out over the field, heading for the farmhouse. As he passed over the gate that joined one field to the lane, he spotted movement in the cab of the tractor he had mentioned to the hare. Spiralling down slowly, he landed with a clattering of claws on the bonnet and glanced in through the window.

A fox looked up at him from the belly of a dead man, his muzzle red and slick with blood. He growled, baring his teeth, his ears flat against his head.

"There's nothing here for you, crow," he snarled.

The crow took off again, leaving the fox to his meal.

"What kept you?" the crow asked from the top of a barrel as Mizieya hopped cautiously into the farmyard.

"I saw a fox and almost ran back the way I'd come," the hare admitted with a shamefaced grin, "but he was busy with something so I managed to sneak past him." He stood up as he had in the field and looked around. "Where is everyone?" he asked.

"I told you, they're dead,"

"You said the men were dead. What about the chickens, ducks and geese? I heard the farmer had goats and cats and a . . . big dog,"

The crow laughed. "So it's the dog you're worried about?" He fluttered down to the ground and walked toward the house itself. "She's still here," he called over his shoulder as Mizieya followed, "but you don't need to worry about her anymore,"

The door of the farmhouse was half open and, with hardly a care in the world, the crow walked in. Looking around, sniffing the air, ears turning this way and that, Mizieya stepped inside.

The house was quiet, dark and heavy with the smell of rotting meat. It took only a moment for the hare's eyes to adjust, but the crow was nowhere to be seen. Instead, two large chairs sat at the end of the room, an extinct fireplace framed between them.

As Mizieya watched, a huge shape rose up from the side of one chair, growling deep in its chest, the dim light picking out its large teeth.

"You're so big and tough, Jessica," the crow said. There was a click as a lamp in one corner lit up, illuminating the scene. Mizieya saw the dog clearly, wincing at the sight of its ribs showing against its flanks; its legs so thin that they trembled with the effort of standing; the skin of it face hanging slack and lifeless as it turned to face the crow.

"I love this thing!" the crow laughed, taking the lamp's chain in its beak and tugging on it. With a click, the light went out, and a second later came on again with another tug. "I can't get enough of this thing!"

"Are you here to torment me again, crow?" Jessica said, sinking to the floor. "And you've brought a friend along as well. Do you have no pity?" She glared at Mizieya.

"How can you say such things, dear Jessie? Young Mizieya here doesn't believe me when I tell him the men are all dead. I though you could convince him."

"Why should I? He's just a hare,"

Mizieya hopped forward, one eye on the crow, the other on Jessica.

"Is it true? Are all the men dead?" he asked. Jessica sighed. "Where are the other animals?"

"Most of them are gone. The chickens, they were just too stupid to survive. The ducks left. So did the geese, the goats and the horses. I feel sorry for the cows," Jessica looked at Mizieya.

"They hadn't been milked for who knows how long. It was all I heard for the first few days: the cries of the cows, calling out to be milked. Eventually, over the last week or so, they stopped one by one. The last one just kept crying 'Please' over and over again. 'Please. Please.' Then she fell silent, too.

"The cats left first. Soon as it happened, they were up and gone. Selfish, really. No loyalty,"

"Unlike you, eh Jessie?" the crow chuckled. "Tell him about the picture box,"

Jessica raised one tired eyebrow at the crow's interruption. "The farmer and his wife used to watch The Telly, the big box in the corner." Mizieya looked over at the television set which sat quiet and dusty, an old lace cloth on its top. "I'm sure the crow will oblige?"

The crow flapped across the room and landed on top of the television. "Jessie told me how to do this," he said, a grin in his voice as he bent over the edge and pushed a large button with his beak.

Before their eyes a picture formed; a row of big old buildings with a large clock tower standing above them. On the roads, burnt out vehicles, cars and buses, lay strewn about, their fires long since extinguished by the rain. Everywhere around them, on the streets and patches of green grass, lay the dead, crumpled in heaps, two or three deep in places.

"It's been showing that same picture for weeks," Jessica said. "I was here with the farmer and his wife as they were watching it. One moment they were talking on The Telly, the next there was a big flash and everyone fell over. Just died where they stood."

"What was it? The flash?" Mizieya asked. Jessica sighed.

"I don't know. For weeks before, the people on The Telly looked unhappy. They gathered at that place, waving sticks and signs, angry about something, that much was obvious. When it happened, I was laying here. The farmer stood up, then fell back down, him and his wife dead like the rest of them. Poor things," Jessica looked up at the two chairs and sighed. Edging closer, Mizieya made out two slumped shapes, one in each chair. From them rose the rich stink of meat left to fester.

"Old Jessie's still guarding them, though, aren't you girl?"

"Get out, crow, and take your friend with you," the old dog said quietly. "I'm tired of telling you this tale. Leave me alone. And turn everything off, too,"

Chuckling, the crow pushed the button on the television then went over to the lamp in the other corner. With a tug on its chain he killed the light, before he flew over to the door. With Mizieya following, the crow walked out into the yard.

"What happened to them?" Mizieya asked. The crow shrugged.

"Who knows? I don't. If anyone around here does it's Jessica, but she's not telling,"

"She's so thin," Mizieya said.

"Yeah, I know. I keep telling her to eat the farmer but she just sits there, talking about loyalty. Me, I'd be fat as - "

The hare stood up suddenly, its nose and ears twitching as it looked around the yard. Bursting from the long grass on the edge of the garden, its mouth still streaked with gore, came the fox.

"Shit!" the crow cried as Mizieya turned to run, colliding with him. As they untangled themselves, the crow frantically flapping over to the safety of the barrel, the fox bit into the hare's neck, flipping him up into the air, grinning as he heard the bones snap.

The Conception
Henrik Jonsson

"Immortal mortals, mortal immortals, live the other's deaths, die the other's lives."

—Heraclitus

I hear her calling to me, late at night; it does not matter that she is dead — her voice still beckons me to sit by her grave and keep her company in the cold, dreary hours of the night. The other inhabitants of the village where I live say I am mad, but little do they know; I have seen the black, abysmal depths into which the human soul sluggishly passes when it has departed from the flesh, and I know she will return to me, even though it has been weeks, months even, since she drew her last breath and I buried her in the garden behind our house, where we had spent so many hours of joy and bliss together. I care not for the whisperings of the villagers; they are of no consequence to me. Mine is not their lot; I am not one of them.

The stone that bears her name is as cold as I fear her touch must be. I chiselled the inscription myself; I would not have anyone else defile her resting-place with their filthy hands. The stone reveals two sets of dates; one, the date of her birth, and the other — I dare not look at it — is that of her death; the day she passed from this world into the next, leaving me alone in this sad, hideous place. The night is as devoid of warmth as the stone, and I wrap my cloak tight around my shoulders. Harsh winds moan fitfully, their cries as plaintive and melancholy as the whispers of decaying corpses. I have in my hand a rose redder than the holiest blood, and I place it on her grave, the grave which I myself dug; as with her tombstone, I would not have it touched by another. Our love was pure and hallowed, as was she on the day we met. I can still recall the dimples on her cheek as she smiled when we were introduced, and I can still remember her teeth, sparkling white and clean, as was she. I knew that she was untouched; I was the first man to taste the sweet, gentle nectar of her love. I recall how much like a goddess of some happier realm she seemed to be on our wedding day, clad all in white and fresh as a petal laden with the dew of a warm summer morning.

I shiver as I touch the dirt of her grave. I know what lies beneath it; her body, and I am filled with revulsion as I imagine what her corpse looks like now — her flesh has decayed, rotted, and melted from her bones like wax held over a flame; her eyes have slowly dissolved into puddles of noxious liquid; her innards have putrefied and are vanishing along with her brain that was so quick and sharp in life; her remains are being consumed by thick, greasy maggots that writhe blindly over her reeking corpse, chewing on her skin, her entrails, her flesh, dissolving what is left of her and growing disgustingly fat on their ghastly diet. The image of a thousand puffy worms burrowing through her rotting flesh fills me with disgust; I am forced to stand up and breathe deeply in order not to faint. With the strength of my will I repel the sickening image from my mind and slowly regain my ease.

And through all the night-tide I sit down by her side, and I once more touch the dirt of her grave, perhaps seeking to be united with her one last time. As I move my hand over the brown earth, I feel her spirit reach out to me; it is as if her love had not died, but had returned from beyond the grave to comfort me. Her grasp is colder than Death himself, but my soul is set ablaze nonetheless. Her clear, blue eyes look longingly at me, and I see them reflected across the skies, looking at me, watching me. Her lips press softly against mine, and we embrace in a passion more fervent and alive than ever we felt in life. Her tongue, not rotted and cold but warm and eager, slithers into my mouth and I taste its forbidden delights; its saliva, sweeter than the purest honey, flows in soft trickles into me and I swallow it, savouring its heavenly flavour.

I place my hand on her neck, burying it underneath her flowing, fragrant hair, which she used to enjoy for me to do when she was still alive; I press her mouth harder against mine and feel her breathpanting heavily against my face. Aroused, I place my hand on her bosom and feel her gently heaving breasts, and I fondle them, and caress them. She is naked, as am I, our clothes removed, and we fondle each other's quivering bodies in a frenzied heat of passion, our lust burgeoning and rising by the instant. I am as a spear of molten lead as I plunge into her, and her warm body welcomes mine. The earth shakes with colossal throes as I pound her flesh, a demon lust flowing through my veins and entering her withered corpse. I scream and the spheres and galaxies scream with me as I lose myself in a whirlwind of unbridled lust, coloured iris and gold with the dust of vanished lovers, where night becomes day as I become her and she melts and becomes me. Lost in a frightful maelstrom of twisted, mad desire, I continue to pound viciously into her rotting, putrescent flesh, and her dissipating entrails are scattered across the grass as the force of my body rocking against hers sways her stinking flesh and twists her sullen, mire-stained corpse into a never-ending phantasmal, contorted vision of infinite obscenity and perverted longing. The stench of her beautiful features melting like butter under a summer sun assails my senses and I laugh as I hear her frail bones snap under my weight. After an eternity of unhallowed passions, my sweat and blood mixing with the noxious puddles left on the ground by her putrid corpse, my anger and love combining with her soft moans of pleasure and forming a heavenly music of suffering and joy, I release my cold seed into the receptacle of her decayed, maggot-filled womb. And then, my energy spent, I bid farewell to my love and fall asleep on the soft, sad earth under which she is buried and forever rests.

The next day, I awake as the sun's harsh light fills the world with its golden glory. I have fallen asleep by the grave of my bride, and the memory of the nightmare I had during the night still clings to me, haunting me. Her grave is untouched, the earth untrod by anyone, least of all by myself. I shed a single tear as I contemplate the joys we shared in life, and then I walk away from her final resting place and enter my abode, seeking solace and comfort, hoping, in vain, to find something that would drive away, if only for a moment, the demons of despair and loneliness that tear at my mind. With strange drugs and stranger magics I have sought to alleviate the melancholy that burdens my soul, but to no avail. Yet I must try once more; and if nothing else, an artificial paradise will provide me with more pleasure than this abysmal wasteland ever can now that my love has left me.

The narcotic fumes from the slowly burning drugs enter me and warp my brain, showing me hidden worlds where creatures prouder and mightier by far than the lowly worms I am ashamed to call my fellow men roam majestic and omnipotent; I soar through skies buried beneath layers of opaque mountains flowing on air as thick as melted diamonds; I see the myriad stars floating through skies blacker than the souls of dead gods, twisting perennially to and fro like a vortex of insane lights and shapes, falling back on themselves and then emerging once more in contours and dimensions that I dare not attempt to comprehend. I fly through some more layers of galaxies and come unto a world of blackness infinite, and there, expecting perhaps to find a few sad dreamers like myself, I see something of such unutterable terror, and yet of such infinite splendour and might; I see the features of my beloved cast against the stars, as if her face had been removed from her body, expanded gigantically and then fastened upon the heavens like a tapestry of never-ending glory. I stretch out my hand to touch her, the one who had once been my soul mate, but she recoils from me,and disappears back into the nothingness where her spirit resides. The terror of her departure shocks me back into this prison of flesh which I am forced to inhabit; I am again made corporeal, and again am I burdened by those demons which torment me endlessly and never let me forget the horror of soul that holds me in its cold embrace.

But I must not succumb to the overwhelming anguish that seeks to drown me in a mire of self-deceit and self-hatred. I must continue with my life; she is dead and I am not, though I often wish it were otherwise — or that I was dead as well, for then I could lie with her in her lightless sanctuary and whisper secrets to her, and we would die eternally, together through the ages, and the worm would not touch us, but we would lie there, loving and laughing in silence until the world ends and the sun loses its warmth. I must go to her again, for I feel her beckoning me to keep her company as she lies there, rotting and vanishing far beneath the earth.

I am by her grave again, as I was last night. I place my hand on her tombstone, and trace the inscription of her name with my finger. It is as if she calls me to do so, and give her some warmth; for, she says, it is cold where she is, down there in the darkness. I pray to whatever god may listen that I shall not suffer such a hideous nightmare as I did on my previous visit; but then, is not life the most terrible and savage dream? I have another flower in my hand, which I now place beside the red rose I gave her last night. The new flower is black, and I do not know its name; but it is pretty, and gives off a sweet scent somewhat reminiscent of sandalwood burning in a basin of darkest marble. Her tendrils stretch out lichen-like as they did yesterday, but I avoid them now, for I know that they do not exist; they are mere ghosts of my fevered imagination come to haunt me in my desolate solitude. I touch her once, and she sighs; then I leave, for happiness as I would enjoy with her is not for me; I am alone, severed from humanity.

I often contemplate joining her in the stillness of the grave; ridding myself of this foul raiment of flesh which constrains me and hinders me from walking among the stars hand in hand with the one my heart cries out to. The knife is sharp and cold; as cold as the wooden box whence it would banish me. Death beckons me to join him in his grey realm, but I bid him to depart and to wait, for some perverse impulse makes me want to continue this mockery of truth called life, hoping beyond hope that I shall some day be reunited with my lost love. Our passion surpassed mortal lust; why should it not be able to reach beyond the grave? The thought strikes me and I gasp with excitement as I suddenly realize that our love is indeed stronger than the bonds that Death imposes on all mortals. I put my mouth to the earth of her grave and tell her of my revelation. She answers and says that I must show her that my love is still pure and true; I must demonstrate my undying affection and devotion to her, and prove that I love her even though she is dead. She tells me that only one thing saddens her, as she lies there rotting in eternity, and that is her inability to bear me a child while she yet lived; her corpse cries bitter tears as she talks to me of how she wants nothing more than to give me a child, so that I may remember her thereby, and by looking at our child, I shall see her face impossibly reflected in the serene features of the fruit of our undying love. Come to me, she says, and show me that you love me still, and I will bear you a child; love me like you did last night, and your solitude shall be banished as our child comes to comfort you in your misery.

I hear you, my most beloved, I reply, and I lay down once more to be united with her, and I cry sweet tears of joy as our flesh is combined into a writhing mass of beautiful obscenity and glamorous hallucinations, and I scream as my body enters hers; I hear her moan with pleasure as I begin to pound her withering corpse, and she whispers words of love and ecstasy which inflame my soul and make beat down on her even harder, crushing her brittle bones and tearing through her parched, leathery skin, and then I laugh and hear her laughing with me as I impregnate her rotting flesh. My dreams are filled with sights forbidden for mere mortals to see, and I walk with her over worlds crowned with reeking porphyry and scintillating, hundred-hued prisms; I tread the stars with her as my master, slave, and lover. We have shattered the bonds of Death with the hammer that is our love, and we are reunited at last. I place my hand on her stomach, and feel the life growing therein.

And once again I awake as the sun shows itself and I shed a few tears as I remember the dream I dreamt during the night, more hideous than the last, more frightful than any other nightmare I have ever had the displeasure of experiencing. I attempt to live a little during the day, but it is impossible. Shreds of the terror induced by the night's reverie clings to my soul and makes my hands tremble; I am unable to prepare any food, and I go through the day famished, anxiously awaiting the night, for I know that something will happen then — I dare not say what, but I am sure that someone, or something, will come and visit me when the sun has fallen, and that this nameless entity shall grant me the bliss I yearn for.

I see the sun setting, and the light slowly fading from the skies. I ready myself for what is to come, but since I know not who or what will visit me tonight, I can only sit in idleness and count the moments slowly vanishing, one after the other. A shadow suddenly passes over my abode, blotting out the last straggling remnants of the sun's light, and I am pitched into darkness more absolute than even the blackness inhabiting my soul. I see nothing, but hear the sound of gigantic wings passing overhead, as if the most terrible of nightmares was flying over me; and I grow even more afraid, for I realize that the shadow is covered by a greater shadow still, and that the blackness surrounding me is but a part of the corruption gathered under the mightiest shadow's demonic wings.

The monstrous shadow departs, and I can see once more, the light of the newly risen moon dimly illuminating my chamber. I hear something on the steps to my abode; the sound of feet walking irregularly across the wooden boards of the porch; but it is oddly distorted, and is more akin to the noise made by metal striking wood. The sound comes nearer, and I hear the front door open, the creaking of its hinges almost, but not quite, masking the steps of the unknown visitor. The footsteps enter my hall, and I am now shivering with the utmost terror. I do not know who or what it is that comes so late in the evening and does not call out to me; I try to convince myself that it is only a burglar come to rob me of my possessions, but I fail.

I wait in silence as the intruder walks across the hall, his feet clicking against the floor. He nears the door of the chamber where I sit, sweating and fearing, and I almost scream with terror as I see the handle of the door being turned; it moves down, and finally the door swings open, not by much, but wide enough to admit into the room an odour so terrible that I gag in disgust. It is the stench of an abattoir reeking with the freshly slaughtered; it is the pungent aroma of lepers, their limbs falling off one by one, the pus from their wounds dripping onto a fire and sizzling evilly; it is the charnel odour of a grave, open and revealing the corpse lodged within for all the world to see. The door is pushed open, and I see something enter the chamber; something that gleams and shines like polished ivory in the moon's silvery light. And now the intruder enters my room and is revealed in all his obscene splendour; it is a skeleton that approaches me, but not the skeleton of a grown man; it is the skeleton of a child.

I see shreds of flesh hanging from its limbs, and I discern the remnants of organs long since melted into oblivion clinging desperately to its spine and ribs; I see its two eyes glaring at me like cold, hard diamonds, their infernal light shining more fiercely than the rays of the evil, gibbous moon. The thing, cloaked in the stench of the newly buried, walks towards me, its skeletal feet clicking on the wooden floor, its eyes focused on my quivering form. A few strands of hair adorn its white scalp, their colour long since faded. The charnel abomination approaches me, and stops a few feet in front of me, standing still, looking at me. I see mirrored within those glassy eyes the fires of unknown hells burning brightly; they are filled with a pain and longing which even I could not dream of. The thing opens its mouth, its jaws creaking as disintegrating sinews are stretched, and it points a bony finger at me, and whispers a word, a word which sends my spirit to be devoured by all the demons of the nether hells; a word which echoes the hideous chanting of my long dead love, her screams of torment issuing from the mouth of her decayed corpse; and what the skeletal child says is merely this — "Father."

The Mutterings of Alyster Austin
Ryhs Hughes

At the request of my friend the editor, I break silence regarding matters he feels me uniquely suited to discuss. Who knows, he, and perhaps you yourself, may request me to resume my silence, having heard it all said better before, or more importantly, you may say, *Quod feci*.

My mentor, Drake, used that phrase a lot. Sat in his living-room, sucking on his pipe, he explained, "It's from Jules Vernes' *Journey to the Centre of the Earth*, where Axel decodes the directions given by the explorer Arne Saknussem. The old boy had written beneath them, *Quod feci*, which freely translates, 'been there, done that'." Drake tapped out his pipe on the hearth.

I took his word for this. My Latin was non- existent. I waited while Drake stuffed his pipe with his usual mixture of donkey shit and toenail clippings before continuing. "I've heard skiploads of half-baked notions of what the centre of the earth must be like, and I bet Verne had too. People believe the weirdest shit-" this from Drake of all people "-and usually they've never been there nor done that. That's beliefs for you. Powerful. Beliefs kick reason, common sense and even experience into touch. Look at the Golden Shower."

The Golden Shower was Drake's name for a hermetic magical society based in the city. When I'd belonged to them I'd found more weird beliefs than you could shake a wand at. You may hear more of these another time.

"Still," Drake went on, through a cloud of acrid blue smoke, "It's not my place to push my beliefs – or disbeliefs – onto you. I daresay you've got enough of your own. What concerns me, boy, is that where your beliefs lead, your life follows. Placebo effect. Doctor tells patient that this medicinal compound will cure his cancer. Cancer disappears. Three months later, patient reads that the medicinal compound doesn't work. Dies in a week. Beliefs. We all have them. Best thing is to choose them carefully."

"Well, yes," I said, "it's important to review the evidence."

"Evidence be buggered! Try telling a born-again Christian about fossils. Evidence is what we use to shore up the beliefs we already hold. Look at Einstein. Quantum mechanics? He wouldn't have it, would he? Said it was unreasonable. 'God does not play dice,' said Albert, as he lay on his back hallucinating flying on light beams." Drake chuckled. "No, boy. You can review the evidence for fossils and stuff. But a belief that really drives your bus is a law unto itself. If you believe you're a piece of shit, that's what you get all your life. People treat you like shit, you get shit jobs, shit places to live, shit happens to you … and there *are* people who believe this of themselves."

He was looking at me with that shifty look of his. "What are you supposed to do?" I asked. "You can't very well say to someone, 'Look, your beliefs are

bad for you: change them.'"

Drake leaned forward in his armchair. "What if you don't?," he said. "The beliefs that run your life are far too powerful to be left to chance. Do that, chances are, you end up with shit. Is that what you want your life to be like? Of course not! So if believing you're a god in plain clothes is what will get you where you want to go in life, you bloody well go and believe it, and argue about the truth of it from a big house called 'Success'."

"But, come on! You can't just change a deeply-felt conviction about yourself."

"My point, boy." Drake was damn nearly out of his armchair by now. "You must, and you can."

"But that sort of thing takes time."

"Only if you listen to some paid-by-the-hour psycho-*anal*-yst. The first belief you could change, boy, is that changing beliefs is difficult. Fix that one and you will change other beliefs at will. *Quod feci.*"

I tried to argue the point with him, but he wouldn't be drawn, saying it was useless to try to reason with beliefs this deeply held. We didn't return to the subject until we had the pool table to ourselves at the Joint & Giro one night. By then I'd done some homework. Or so I thought. Talking above the dated pop music I got as far as "I've been looking into some ideas about changing beliefs."

"Theories, you mean? I told you before, boy; I can't be arsed with theories." Drake smacked the cue ball into the triangular pack, sending the balls all over the table and potting a yellow one. "Theories are only good for arguments. Saw two Buddhists get into a

fight once. The Chinese one believed that the human energy field runs in channels around the body. The Indian one believed that energy was located in chakras. There's this ball of energy above the crown of your head-" he gestured vaguely, using the hand that held the chalk "-then there's a ball of energy at the throat, the chest, all the way down to your bum." Drake surveyed the table. "That's a lot of balls. Funny thing was, both of those guys could do amazing things with their balls. Or channels." He bent over the table, lining up a shot. "These ideas of yours: which ones have you tried?"

"Tried?"

"Right. None of 'em." Drake sighed, then slammed a yellow ball into a corner pocket, screwing the cue ball practically back to the cue tip. He lined up again, barely shifting position. "Come on then, tell me what they are."

"Well, it's a fact that new information can change the way we see things ..."

Drake sent a yellow ball trickling into a side pocket. "Grant you that. How long does it take?"

"How long?"

"Does the word 'eureka' mean anything to you?" Drake nudged a yellow ball over a corner pocket.

I started to line up a shot. "Sudden realization-" I stood upright. "That fast?"

"All it takes is for some new variable to enter the equation, and in the time it takes for the penny to drop-" Drake paused. "Play your shot."

I bent back down over the table, lined up. Drake continued, "The trick then, is to know the techniques to get the penny to drop."

"Well, there's mind-expanding drugs..." I missed

my shot. Drake grinned as he took over.

"And the Death Posture and many other trance states. The good news is, they each amplify your state of mind, which makes belief implantation easier. The bad news is, they amplify any shit, which means if you're vague and grasshoppering through lots of weak ideas, that's what you'll implant." He left another yellow over a pocket. "Which accounts for the crystals-and-didgeridoos crap that comes out of prats like Cosmic."

"Okay. Then there's affirmation," I said, quickly potting an easy red.

"Ah yes. Goebbels method. Tell the same lie often enough for long enough, people will believe it. Similar to fake-it-till-you-make-it. Works, just takes too long." He bent down next to me as I lined up my next red. "Rehearse it in trance and it sinks in more quickly." I potted my red. "Next?"

I went for an ambitious shot. "One thing I have tried in the past is to suspend judgement. It's a bit like going to see a film and suspending your disbelief. You can watch the film without reminding yourself that it's all made up."

For a change, Drake looked impressed. And yes, I did pot the ambitious red. "So," he said, "you drop all attempts to rationally justify your chosen belief and you deliberately ignore any evidence to the contrary."

"Yes," I answered, quickly cuing a shot and glancing at Drake. "It's what we seem to do to implant beliefs the rest of the time, after all."

"You haven't explained yet how these methods remove beliefs,' Drake said. 'For a deeply

dysfunctional self-image, you're going to need more than a bunch of affirmations and a lot of make-believe." He glanced at the cue ball, which was rolling merrily into a yellow ball, which in turn dropped into a pocket. "That's two shots."

A guy in a lumberjack shirt put some change on the edge of the table as Drake walked around the table to his next shot. "You think of an absolute conviction you have. Is the sun rising tomorrow, Al?"

I nodded. Drake smiled. "Course it is." He potted another yellow. "Now think of believing in Father Christmas. Ho ho ho jingle bells. Get each of those clear in your head. Good. Now think of a belief you wish you didn't have, bad self-image shit. Got it?"

Again, I nodded, Drake potted.

"Make that belief exactly similar to believing in Father Christmas. Bad self-image shit ho ho ho jingle bells." BANG! Drake slammed in a yellow. "Now do it again a few times."

I did as I was told. "Okay," he said, running a slow yellow diagonally into a corner pocket, "create a belief you'd like to have, maybe that you're a god going incognito. My favourite self-image. Got it in your mind? Good. Now make it exactly similar to believing that the sun is rising tomorrow. God going incognito? Course it is." Drake lined up the black. BANG! middle pocket. . "Now do that a few times quickly." He stood up from the table, grinning. "Good game."

Drake made it seem so simple. Anyway, I invite your response to these mutterings of mine. But please, I do not wish you to regale me with your beliefs, however special and privileged you may really feel them; rather, ask me questions and tell me your adventures of choosing beliefs which take you where you want to go. And may whatever you call success follow. *Quod feci.*

Karma Codswallop

Rhys Hughes

The same mistake reborn in a new shell: that is the closest fiction will come to authentic reincarnation. Because the concept is illogical. Never to be lightly discouraged by insurmountable obstacles on the single path through the labyrinth of abstraction, too many fantasy writers are still unable to grasp that the basic idea of the nomad soul setting up camp in a selection of bodies has no validity at all. It is wrong by definition. A small examination of the issues, and tissues, might suffice to keep it in its place, under lock and key of bone and muscle. The spirit does not exist, but even if it did, there is no migration ahead for it. Where the flesh putrefies, so must identity.

When it comes to invented cases, the major prophet of this subgenre remains Rider Haggard. His fatalistic character, She-Who-Must-Be-Obeyed, must eventually learn to hide her disappointment, in the sense that at least one of her whims can never be obeyed. She orders her new lover, Leo Vincey, to accept the fact he was also her paramour in a remote time, indeed that she has been waiting for him all these centuries. He falls for it. His utter contempt for logic is typical of the breed of hero found in most adventure tales, speculative or not, by Haggard (King Solomon's Mines (1885) features the strangest solar eclipse in literature, occurring immediately between two full moons on three successive nights), or by his imitators, even now, in our supposedly less callow age.

Prime offender, despite, or perhaps because of, his atmospheric and rococo imagination, Edwin Lester Arnold turned serial reincarnation into an acceptable theme for any writer with an interest in comparative bogus history. His first novel, Phra the Phoenician (1890), sets the stiffness and mysticism for much that followed, losing its way early and so giving the others no chance. Phra tries different lives in a selection of eras, jumping from his original form as a slave in Ancient Britain to his last earthly sojourn in the reign of Queen Elizabeth, a karmic tour taking in regular periods between. At least he keeps his real body, safely hidden, in a state of mummification, ready to receive his itinerant spirit. This is a rather important detail. He comes to a charming, awkward end, equal to the solecisms of his own prose.

No matter. The glut was extreme but seemingly finite. The clumsy Ziska (1897) by Marie Corelli still has not shared the destiny of its main protagonist, and is unlikely to, for the chance of a reprint is mercifully slight. More gibberish with single lifetimes include A Son of Perdition (1912) by Fergus Hume, Avernus (1924) by Mary Bligh Bond, When They Came Back (1938) by Roy Devereux and I Live Again (1942) by Warwick Deeping, timid variations on an identical flaw. More stubborn than most, Virginia Woolf's Orlando (1928) is a transparent excuse to meddle with a character's gender to relieve the author's own sexual frustrations. Such remedies rarely work, and here the context is boring. Only Jack London's crack at the fallacy, The Star Rover (1915), is redeemed by anarchic and fretful writing. A capital fellow.

The problem in the theme, as always, is one of strict definition. A person's soul might be regarded as the essence of their personality, and the body as a house or vehicle for its conveyance. Thus rigid parameters for this material vessel are deemed irrelevant. It is less of what a man or woman is than their hypothetical spirit. When the eponymous cleric in Lord Dunsany's My Talks With Dean Spanley (1936) dimly remembers his former existence as a dog, it is clear that readers are supposed to believe the true core of an individual, his or her identity, remains uninfluenced by its own interaction with the shape which currently holds it, an attitude which reveals monumental ignorance about the nature of mind and self. It can hardly be overstressed that an identity is not just the sum of ideas and memories featured in a single mind, corporeal or otherwise, but also is determined by variable factors such as societal context, the concepts and emotions of other people, space and time, relationships and customs, most of all: contemporary language.

It makes absolutely no sense for a Phra dwelling in the year of the Spanish Armada to assert that he was once also a Phra who fought for the Roman Legions as a centurion, and later at Hastings as yet another Phra, to say nothing of the Saint Phra who earned his beatification in the era of Edward III. Much better to state that what is happening here are five wholly separate lives, which only a convergence of personal tastes seems to have linked. The connection is an illusion. To construct an elaborate theory of transmigration of souls on these imaginary bonds is opposed to all rules of logic and decency. There ought

chunk of the ego is *external*, shaped by interaction with elements of the human world. Exactly what one *is* can never be determined in isolation, for it is partly a product of what the minds which react with an individual believe. Consciousness is behaviour no less than intellect, neither objective nor subjective but between the pair. The ego is *inter-subjective*, influenced by the ideas, opinions and actions of others. There are no private or unique thoughts, only private and unique ways of arranging ideas which already exist. To proclaim unity and congruence of identity for a sprinkling of Phras in space-time is a non-sequitur of numbing duplicity.

Napoleon was Napoleon not simply because he believed himself to be, but equally because a majority of other people agreed with his analysis. The lunatic in the asylum who imagines himself to be Napoleon will never be him. Even if he convinces a majority of his fellow patients, doctors, the wider public, of this assertion, he still lacks the circumstances of the real Napoleon's life, the original body, the wife, the civilisation, the atmosphere, the chronology, the *context*. Napoleon's ego was invented not just by himself, but by his contemporaries, and now also by us. Else he would not exist in the form he has. It is hard enough playing oneself successfully, let alone trying to assume the identity of someone else. A lunatic who suddenly found himself possessed of Napoleon's memories, his desires and ambitions, his quirks of character and education, still must define himself by his own identity. The most that can be said is that he has become like Napoleon, perhaps even exactly alike, but that condition is far from a state of *being* him. Even exactly alike, odd as this seems, will always lack the rigour of *is*.

Thus She-Who-Must-Be-Obeyed is fated to settle for second best, for Leo Vincey, despite his ostensibly antique feelings, is only a very close, perhaps exact, simulacrum of the original. Without rebuilding its utter context to every atom, he remains a replacement, despite parity of attitude, lips, wallet, whatever features first attracted her, all those empires ago. Haggard is haggard, in two senses, but all is not yet lost. One of the very few fictional treatments of reincarnation worth pursuing for a sophisticated plot based genuinely on the notion of transmigration of souls, and cliches, is *Men of Maize* (1949) by the Guatemalan novelist Miguel Angel Asturias. Those smart objections to reincarnation which now have made further use of the theme in fantasy literature inept and inadmissible apply only to rebirths of identity. Reoccurring non-ego selves have slicker formats. When the *atman* is removed from the formula, a mystery really might return as an enigma.

Unrecommended Reading:

Transmigration (1874)......Mortimer Collins

Lepidus the Centurion (1901)......Edwin Lester Arnold

The Yellow God (1908)......Rider Haggard

The Bridge of Time (1919)....William Henry Warner

The Man who was Born Again (1921)......Paul Busson

The Three Gentlemen (1932)......A.E.W. Mason

Alas, That Great City (1948)....Francis Ashton

Your Turn

Mark McLaughlin

She sweeps toward you, laughing, her lace-swathed arms outstretched. She is the Red Nurse and she is about to put her large hot hands on you.

So you run, because you know no one survives her brand of care. You see a small blue house with all the lights on and toys scattered in the front yard. The Red Nurse abhors children so you hurry up to the door and start knock-knock-knocking. Oh please, let all the horrible children be home.

The door glides open and a beautiful young Asian man with platinum hair takes you by the hand and wordlessly leads you inside. You slam the door behind you and command the young man to lock it. He shrugs and does as he is told.

In the kitchen, he makes you a peanut butter and jelly sandwich. *"Say* something," you insist. "I'm being chased by the Red Nurse and I want you to take my mind off her."

"Well, let me think," he says. "How about this? My name is Peter. My mother is French and my father is Japanese but I never knew him. I'm making you a P, B & J because it has a lot of fat and sugar and protein in it and those are all good things to eat when you're scared. So here, eat this. Want some milk?"

You nod and take the sandwich. You watch as Peter picks up an empty glass from the counter and turns around. Time passes. He's just standing there *doing* something, but you can't see what. So you watch and eat and watch. Finally he turns around and hands you a full glass.

The glass is fridge-cold and filled with a white liquid.

"What is this stuff?" you ask, eighty-five percent disgusted, ten percent amused, five percent intrigued.

"It's milk," Peter says.

"No it's not. It came out of you."

"Well, yeah. It's my milk."

You look him up and down. "What did it come out of?"

He brushes his fingers along your jawline. "If the Red Nurse catches you, you'll never have any milk ever again."

Something jumps up on the counter, startling you - you almost drop the milk. At first you think it's a cat, but it's too big, and it's a biped, and it's wearing a gold mask and a black rubber suit crisscrossed with zippers, and you suddenly realize it's the Cat Man, and you KNOW that the Cat Man is a very good friend of the Red Nurse, and you turn toward Peter and shout, "Is this a trap?"

He puts his hands on your face and says, "No, no, no, calm down, the Cat Man is mad at the Red Nurse and he's staying with me. He's the one who put all the toys in the front yard. Pretty smart, huh?"

You face the Cat Man. "How do I know this isn't a double-cross? Why are you mad at the Red Nurse?"

"She lied to me." His soft little voice sounds like a big tree growing. "She promised me Australia and India and most of Africa and all I got was Hawaii. I mean, Hawaii is pretty and all, but I was expecting a lot more. We had a deal. Hey, if you're not going to finish that, can I have it?"

You let the little guy have your sandwich. He removes his mask to eat and you almost pass out because his face is so ugly (pale damp flesh, protruding blue-green veins, watery golden eyes). He eats like a frenzied boarhog, grunting and heaving and gurgling as he chews.

Peter taps his chin thoughtfully. "So Cat Man. What's the plan? How you gonna get back at her? What sort of nasty trick do you have up your black rubber sleeve?"

The little guy flashes a slick grin. "Tell ya what. You two help me and I'll cut you in. Petey, you can have France and Japan and any ten of the fifty states of America. And you, Scaredy Pants: you can have Germany and Argentina and any ten states, too - but Petey gets first pick. Is it a deal?"

You wonder why your mouth tastes like oranges. Then you realize that while the Cat Man was talking, you drank the whole glass of Peter-milk.

It takes days of cool persuasion and heated negotiation, but finally the Cat Man and Peter convince you to join in on the scheme. It takes so long because they won't tell you what the sheme is.

Peter leads the way down into the murky basement. At the Cat Man's command, he fills a laundry bag with things from a big wooden crate under he stairs. You aren't quite sure what the things are, but they look like black books or boxes.

The Cat Man hangs the Seal Of Wounds That Won't Heal on the handle of the old furnace's heavy metal door. He swings the door open and you find yourself looking into one of the ultra-white corridors of the House of the Ankh. In you all crawl, one, two, three.

"That was easy," you say.

The Cat Man waves a blacknailed hand dismissively. "Getting into trouble is always easy." He reaches back into the opening and pulls out the Seal, closing the way behind him.

"Why did you do that?" you whisper hotly into his damp triangular ear. "That was our escape hatch!"

Suddenly an Iguana Man guard rounds the corner of the hall. The Cat Man pulls a wee gun out of one of his many pockets and shoots the reptile between the eyes. The silencer is almost as big as the gun, so the shot only makes a tiny pfffft!

"Hatch schmatch," the Cat Man hisses. "What a big wetsy baby you are. Let's get moving."

You help Peter carry the sack as you follow the little guy through the winding halls. On both sides of you: walls dotted with framed certificates (there's one signed by Hitler) and doors, doors, doors, hundreds of them, all white, some slightly ajar. Every now and then you peek into one of the rooms. In the various rooms you see: locusts feasting on exposed brains; looping, living guts stuck with glowing pins; orifices crammed with gardening implements; and you keep saying to yourself, Italy, they promised me Italy.

In all these rooms, set high up on the walls are video monitors, all playing exotic, brightly-lit torture scenes. For ambiance, perhaps, like music in elevators.

At last you come to a door guarded by two Iguana Men. The Cat Man plugs them both with his tiny gun before they even have a chance to reach for their weapons. Dying, one of the guards shits his pants, filling the hall with an eye-watering ammonia stench.

The room you now enter is huge, and filled with computer stations. Each station features a bluish-gray zombie, staring at a monitor and typing. A cable runs from the side of each monitor to the base of the spine of its zombie-typist.

"Here we are," the Cat Man says. "Took a little longer than I thought to find it. She changes the location of this room constantly."

"Is this the nerve-center of operations?" you ask.

The little guy shakes his damp head. "Nah, this is just where they play the torture videos."

Each zombie is wearing a black burlap shirt. The Cat Man rips the shirt off the nearest zombie, revealing a square slot in the middle of its back. He presses a button by the slot and a video cassette pops out.

Peter opens the sack and takes out a video labeled SWEDISH HOT-TUB DUDES, which he slides into the zombie-slot. One by one, he replaces the torture videos in all the zombies with selections from his porn library.

"Is this the big plan?" you say, exasperated. "Why did you two even bother to get me involved? You didn't need me at all!"

The Cat Man takes your hand and tugs gently downward. You kneel to look him in the eye. "You, my friend," he says, "play a vital role in this curious enterprise. A starring role. Starting now."

He unzips one of his many zippers, reaches in and pulls out a sort of collar, studded with small gems and computer chips. You want to look at it more closely, but before you can, he snaps it around your neck.

From another of his pockets he pulls an oval device covered with buttons. He points the thing at you and presses a big red button.

And now you are a woman, or at least, female: the Green Nun.

Of course, the name is all part of the joke. After all, the Red Nurse isn't really a nurse. Most nurses like to cure people, not chop them into bits. And while nuns aren't supposed to like sex, *you* certainly don't have a problem with it.

Like the Cat Man, you wear a skintight, many-zippered rubber suit - yours is lime-green, with a yellow and blue swirly pattern over the breasts. You don't wear a mask, but you do cover your face with a bridal veil.

The revolution was a success: the energy from the torture rooms - the secret source of the Red Nurse's power - has been channeled away from her and into you. And you feel *fantastic*.

Your first order of business was to give the Cat Man a kiss and a big hug. Then you twisted off his smelly head. You confiscated the remote (as if he could ever control *you*), that tiny little gun, and of course, the Seal of Wounds That Won't Heal, along with the other goodies in those deceptively deep pockets of his. You commanded your new guards, the Tarantula Men, to seize and detain Peter. Then you shifted the location of the zombie room to a transdimensional bunker in Q Sector. There's no air in Q Sector, but the zombies won't mind.

In the Imperial Boudoir, you watch as the Tarantula Men strip off Peter's clothes. You raise an eyebrow at the sight of his convoluted genitalia.

"You were supposed to save us!" Peter cries.

"I <u>am</u> saving you. For myself."

You press a green button on the nightstand and a silver communications monitor rises out of the floor. The screen lights up to reveal the bristly face of the Head Tarantula Man.

"Any word on the Red Nurse?" you roar.

His mandibles tremble. "She has escaped the grounds. Six-dozen death-squads are out searching. We think she has found her way into the Swamplands."

"The Swamplands! But - that's where the Resistance is headquartered!"

You grab a crystal dildo out of your curio cabinet and fling in at the screen. The monitor explodes in a shower of shards and sparks.

Out of the corner of your eye, you see Peter yawn. *Yawn?* How enraging! "Am I *boring* you?"

He smiles apologetically, then nods to the left and right at the Tarantula Men holding him. "Maybe we should talk. But first, get rid of your goons. You wouldn't want them to hear what I have to say."

You command the guards to chain him to the bed.

They do as they are told and depart.

Peter stretches out on the mattress. For a prisoner, he seems awfully unconcerned. "I really envy you," he says. "You get so far into it, you can actually forget what's going on."

His words disturb you, and yet you say, "Continue."

"You. Me. Her. The three of us." He taps his chin. "I used to be the Purple Queen. You were the Brown Hunter. She was the Yellow Bishop. Then I was the White Dollmaker. You were the Blue Shaman. She -"

You turn away. "*Enough!* I don't have time for these games."

"No," he says, "that's the problem. We have too much time, and only for games."

You think about this for a moment. Then you sigh. "Say whatever else you've got to say."

"I love you. But I love her, too. Even though she doesn't care about me." He laughs softly. "She's still wild about you. And we're *never* sure how you feel about either of us! It's sad, really, and so very tedious. But at least we have our games! Tricks and terrors, puzzles and perversions. They make it all seem so glamorous."

You turn back to him, wiping at your eyes with the veil. "I think I liked it better when we were -" Were what? What? "- playing."

"Well, then," he says "let's keep playing. But bring back the Cat Man. I made him the last time I was evil, and ... well, the game's more interesting when he's around. He's so deliciously treacherous."

You give him a small nod. Then you push another button on the nightstand and a new communications monitor rises out of the floor.

You square your shoulders. "Reanimate the Cat Man's corpse," you thunder, "and bring him to my antechamber."

Peter's reflection beams at you from the rounded silver edge of the monitor. How happy he looks. You open a door on the nightstand and bring out a corkscrew and a magnum of passionflower wine. Before long, you and your handsome prisoner are laughing and taking swigs from the big bottle.

There is a knock on the door. You purr, "Be back in a second," and then glide away from the bed. At one point, you glance back and give Peter a wink.

You enter your antechamber, where a Tarantula Man waits, holding the Cat Man in his arms. The little guy's head has been reattached, but he is still extremely groggy.

You open one of your zippers and take out a gold pill case and a shiny greenish-blue sliver of metal. The case holds a single hyperstrength super-energy pill, which you slip under the Cat Man's tongue. Then you slide the metal sliver - a cerebral implant - deep into his damp triangular ear.

These words you whisper into that ear: "Go into the next room, straight to the bed. There you will find a chained man and a stainless steel corkscrew. Use the corkscrew to remove the man's brain, a little bit at a time."

You smile to yourself. Pretty, silly Peter. You still can't believe that your false tears fooled him. Bored? Soon he will be bored out of his skull! Serves him right for acting so damnably sincere, so *real*. Ordinarily you like that sort of thing, but not when it's your turn to be the evil one.

Growing Pains

Paul Lewis

Stanton sprawled naked on his bed, miserably contemplating what he had come to think of as The Enemy. It hung there limply, as it had done for months. He frowned as he stared down, almost as if willpower alone could resurrect it.

On the bedside table was a small framed photograph of Tina, all that remained to suggest she had once shared his life. A solitary, slightly blurred snapshot. Her face, so hard when she walked out, was captured for ever in softer tones.

She had been sympathetic when it had first happened. One of those things, she'd said, convinced it was temporary. But in spite of her gentle coaxings and imaginative ministrations, his condition did not improve.

He still did not know what was causing his impotence, and there was no way on God's earth he was going to see the doctor, as Tina had begged. Some things a man had to resolve for himself; the prospect of some newly-qualified medical hotshot fiddling with his equipment was one he flatly refused to entertain. Give it enough time and the problem would sort itself out. He hoped.

So it continued, for nearly six months, until the day he came home to find Tina gone. They had fought the previous night, Tina screaming he was too busy getting it up for someone else to have strength left for her. She had even searched his clothes for evidence while he watched in silence. He knew her leaving was enough to tell him he needed help - professional help - but he still could not bring himself to act.

Then for some reason he found himself thinking about Peggy Hall.

The cottage stood on a bend of the lane which snaked up the hillside above Bethesda. Sunlight flared in the windows and made the whitewashed walls shimmer, but this did not disguise the fact that the place was badly in need of repair. A couple of roof tiles were missing and the garden was overgrown, choked with weeds.

Stanton paused at the bottom of the cracked steps which led from the lane to the cottage, calves aching, chest on fire. It was a bright November day and even though the air was cold, he was sweating. Christ, was he out of shape.

He could not believe he was doing this, wanted to turn round and go straight back home. What did he hope to gain? There was only the slightest chance Tina had contacted the woman. Then again, a small chance was better than none. Stanton was not sure how much longer he could bear the total breakdown of communication that existed between him and his estranged wife.

And if Mrs Hall had not heard from Tina, at least she might be of a mind to talk a little while, perhaps suggest a couple of places where Tina could have gone.

She was Tina's aunt, after all.   "So," Peggy Hall said. "You and Tina are going through a bad patch. Sugar?"

The non-sequitur threw Stanton. For a moment he thought she had meant it as a term of endearment. "No. No thanks."

"Right." The old woman's hands were steady as she poured tea into two fragile-looking cups decorated with painted flowers. "I hope you don't mind Earl Grey," she said pleasantly. "More refreshing, don't you find?"

"Definitely," Stanton mumbled. In truth, he didn't know the difference between Earl Grey and PG Tips. Still, it never hurt to be polite.

He studied his host and realised he had never seen her close-up before. It was not as if he had ever deliberately avoided her but it seemed their paths had never crossed, other than at a distance. Strange that, in a village the size of Bethesda.

Mrs Hall was not as old as he had imagined. Mid-sixties, maybe. She wore a bright, floral-patterned dress which, while loose, could not disguise her trim figure. There were laughter lines around her mouth and eyes, which would flash now and then with a mischievous sparkle. She looked like someone's favourite grannie.

Another surprise; the cottage may have looked run-down from the outside but its interior was neat and clean. The living room in which they sat was dominated by a huge oak unit, its shelves lined with rows of books. Stanton tried to read the titles but they were too distant for him to see clearly. There was a

mantelpiece laden with brass ornaments, and an unlit gas fire. The room smelled strongly of air freshener.

Mrs Hall handed him a cup which he held carefully as if afraid it would shatter at the slightest pressure. He tasted the tea; it was hot and strong and carried the faintest suggestion of herbs.

"I was asking about Tina," the old woman said as she sat on a chair opposite.

"You haven't heard from her?"

Mrs Hall raised a carefully-plucked eyebrow. "Me? My dear, what makes you think I would have heard from her?"

"You're her aunt."

"Great-aunt, actually. She's my nephew's daughter. And no, I haven't heard from her. We didn't see much of each other even when she was living in Bethesda."

"Then how did you know we were going through a bad patch?"

"You get to hear everything in this place," she said, and laughed. Then her face grew serious. "If you want

to talk about your problem, I'm a good listener."

Stanton shook his head. "There's no point, if you haven't heard from her."

"I didn't mean Tina. I meant your other problem."

He nearly choked on his tea. No way she could have known about his impotence, not unless Tina had told her. And she reckoned they had not spoken. He stared at her, wondering if she had lied, then made to stand. "If you do hear from Tina, I'd be grateful if you'd ask her to get in touch with me."

"Oh, sit down," Mrs Hall said, placing a restraining hand on his knee. "Nothing you say could possibly embarrass me, young man. All we need to do is get to the root of the problem, then we can see about solving it."

"Everything's fine," Stanton insisted.

"Then why did you come to see me?"

Stanton shrugged. No matter what she knew about his condition, he was hardly going to sit there and ask what he had to do to get a hard-on again.

Which, later, was more or less what he found himself asking.

He was back home, sitting on the bed, contemplat-

ing the doll he had propped against Tina's photograph, not knowing what the hell to think.

Doll is what Mrs Hall had called it. To Stanton it simply looked like a small piece of wood, bundles of twigs vaguely representing arms and legs tied to it with twine. At the base of the wood - the torso - was a small bump. Stanton wondered exactly what that was supposed to represent.

It's you. Believe in it.

That's what she'd said, old Peggy Hall. In fact she'd said a lot of things, none of them of much interest to Stanton, who had sat in silent mortification after admitting for God knows what reason that, yes, he was impotent. When she told him she could help, he assumed she would give him the name of a doctor or therapist she knew. If she had done that then maybe he would have taken up the suggestion, just to keep her happy. Instead she had given him the doll. And instructions on how to use it.

Stanton had felt his cheeks burn when she described what he needed to do. What was the word

he had used? Activate it, yes. She had used the word seed a couple of times, which made him think vaguely of gardening. But what she was saying, quaint metaphors aside, was that he would have to masturbate over the thing.

Fine, he thought. Just fine and fucking dandy.

Question was - and he actually asked this, God help him - how the hell was he supposed to achieve that magnificent act in his present state?

It's you, was her reply, simply stated. Believe in it.

What a waste of time! It was only later, as he paused to catch his breath after jogging down the hill, that he realised he was still clutching the doll.

He felt more depressed than ever. The midday sun had given way to heavy clouds. Rain drenched the village. Only three o'clock and already the bedside lamp was on. Stanton glared at the doll, as if blaming it for the weather. It was pathetic, really. A child could do better. No doubt Peggy Hall was pissing herself right now, having a right old laugh at his expense as she imagined her great-niece's soon-to-be ex-husband wanking off over it. No way, he thought.

And then it happened. The tinniest stirring, the faintest suggestion of life in the old boy. Not much, but it was a damn sight more than he had felt in months.

He looked at the doll again, feeling oddly uneasy which in turn made him feel slightly stupid. It was bullshit. Bits of wood were not exactly up there with Viagra as the world's number one cure for impotency. Yet he could not help but wonder what might happen if, against his better judgement, he followed the instructions.

He could not believe what he was contemplating. Then again, what if the doll really did work? What did he have to lose? He was alone in the house. Alone in the world, come to that. Nobody would see him. Nobody would know. And if he had been taken for a ride ... well, apart from feeling like an idiot there would be no harm done.

And there it was again. A definite throbbing this time.

Stanton mulled it over for a moment. Then he reached out for the doll.

Stanton could hear music thumping faintly through the walls of the stationery cupboard. The party was in full swing in the general office just down the corridor. They were safe enough in here, even with the door unlocked, unless someone felt a drunken urge to go fetch some paperclips.

As Michelle's sweat-slicked body writhed under his, Stanton recalled a time when he used to consider work boring. He would drive on autopilot along the main road to Cardiff, yawn as he hunted down a space in the multi-storey, sit at his desk, and wipe away sleep as he made a start on the in-tray. He would attend meetings, stop now and then to chat to the girls in the typing pool, return to his desk, check the time.

At five he would leave, swear as he battled the rush-hour traffic, arrive home, eat, watch TV, go to bed and sleep until it was time for the cycle to repeat itself.

Not any more. These days work was fun.

He was over Tina. He could go days at a time without her face springing to mind when he least expected it. And when it did, it no longer hurt.

No sir. There was more than enough happening to make up for Tina.

Single women, divorced women, married women. Hotels, motels, car seats, occasionally his own office. Admittedly he had never used the stationery cupboard before and the pain in his elbows reminded him not to try that one again. Never mind. At least now he could strike Michelle from his mental list of conquests.

Later, as they prepared to rejoin the party, she said: "Know what? It's true what they say about you."

Stanton straightened his tie. "What do they say about me?"

"You're big," said Michelle. "That's what they say."

He considered himself a tender lover, an experienced lover, certainly a talented lover. But never had he thought of himself as being big. "Oh?"

"They're right," Michelle sighed. "Biggest I've had. Ever."

He turned to face her and she pressed her lips against his. Her hand dropped to his thigh and she cupped him through his trousers. Stanton, thinking she was right, he was bloody big, decided the party could wait.

He woke late on New Year's Day, hot and sweaty and shaking with fever. He was alone. Michelle had been fun but he had tired of her by Boxing Day. He had spent last night propping up the bar in the Globe, the sole pub in the village. His mates had been there and between them they had disposed of an inordinate amount of beer.

Stanton had a distant memory of the televised chimes of Big Ben but his mind was a blank after that.

He felt ill yet not hung-over. Time to get up, check the mirror for damage. Stanton threw back the quilt and sweat-soaked sheet, dragged his legs across to the side of the bed -

And gasped in sudden pain.

He moved his hand down to his groin and was rocked by another wave of hot, shooting agony. His eyes screwed shut, his teeth clenched. Fresh perspiration broke out all over him. He lay still. By the time the pain subsided he was too afraid to move.

He lowered his hand again, gently this time, but even so his fingers had the same effect as red-hot needles when they brushed against the swelling. Stanton wanted to scream. He clamped his mouth shut, tasting copper and salt as his teeth nipped his tongue but feeling nothing beyond that sheer Christ-awful pain.

It was an age before he could breathe again. An eternity before he could bring himself to look down. "Oh sweet Jesus," he whispered.

The Enemy was twice its normal size. It looked red and angry and liable to burst if he touched it. Then it pulsed. No, not pulsed. It actually grew. Right before his fucking eyes it actually, visibly grew. Stanton felt sick. The thing had expanded to at least twice its normal size, and apparently it had not finished growing yet.

This was something he really would have to talk to his doctor about. At least he could request a home visit without feeling guilty. All he had to do was get out of bed, walk down the stairs and into the lounge where the phone was. He could do it. If he was careful and took his time, he could do it. At least he would not have to make the return journey. He could sit himself downstairs and wait.

And while he was waiting he would think about what to say when the doctor arrived. He could hardly claim celibacy. Equally there was no reason why he should reveal the full extent of his conquests. Fine. He had slept with a few women and one of them had passed him more than a post-coital cigarette. God, if only he had stayed impotent. If he hadn't gone to see Peggy Hall, if he hadn't -

He remembered the doll, feeling embarrassed and disgusted when he recalled what he had done with it. But he was certain of one thing. Regardless of his actions, the doll had not made any difference. It had not been activated. It was just a piece of wood and he had thrown it into the garden shed with all the other rubbish.

Enough of that for now. He had work to do.

Getting downstairs was a nightmare. He wore a loose dressing gown but no matter how much care he took, he could not prevent the thing slapping against his legs now and then. When that happened he would freeze, his face a rictus of agony, until he was able to move again. One hand gripped the banisters, the other was pressed against the wall opposite. He could not afford to slip.

Finally he was down.

The telephone sat on a small table in a corner of the lounge. Stanton eased himself into the armchair nearest it. He made himself as comfortable as possible, waited until his breathing and heartbeat had settled. He picked up the receiver, almost dropped it, then pressed it to his ear. He was not surprised to find there was no dialling tone. He looked out the window at the grey afternoon sky, noticed for the first time how heavily the snow was falling. Weather must have brought the lines down.

No way could he walk to the doctor's house. Driving was equally out of the question. He could hobble around to one of the neighbouring houses, of course, but what in Christ was he going to say? He almost laughed, except it hurt too much.

Stanton was cold but the central heating switch was in the kitchen and he couldn't face moving just yet. Maybe later. Perhaps he would feel a little stronger. Or perhaps the swelling might go down. Unlikely, that. If anything it was getting worse.

He groaned. Despite all that was happening to him he could not get that stupid doll ou and for all. At least then he could concentrate on the practical business of summoning medical help.

Stanton nodded, mind made up. He eased himself out of the chair and shuffled into the kitchen, flicking the central heating switch down as he passed. At least it would not be cold in here when he returned from the garden. He debated putting on something warmer but in the end decided that would take too long and no doubt be too painful. He shouldn't be out more than ten minutes, even with limited mobility.

The cold hit him as he opened the back door. It was still snowing and the wind had picked up. Flakes flew into his eyes, half-blinding him. The afternoon gloom was pressing in, a stillness broken only by occasional passing vehicles; these sounded muffled, distant. Trees and high hedges shielded him from his neighbours, which was just as well. He was still holding the dressing gown away from him, and walking like a zombie. God alone knew what he would look like to any observer.

Stanton stepped gingerly onto the white lawn. The shed was at the far end. It seemed the length of a football pitch away. The wind-swirled snow created the illusion of a tunnel, and crunching ice beneath his feet made him think of broken limbs. He tested the ground with each step before putting his full weight down.

Cold. Too cold. He had only been outside a minute or so and already his blood had seemingly turned to ice. He had never experienced anything like it. Stanton closed his eyes, willed himself to take one pace, then another. The pain in his groin was hideous but he closed his mind to it. He forced himself to think about Tina, and before long his agony felt like it belonged to someone else.

He reached the shed, fumbled at the latch with numb hands. For a moment he thought it had frozen up but the door swung open and he stumbled inside. He could do nothing but stand shivering violently for several minutes. His hands and face tingled unpleasantly as feeling returned. Finally he was able to move again. And immediately wished he hadn't. The Enemy began to burn.

Stanton slammed his hand against his mouth to prevent himself from screaming. His eyes filled, his vision blurred. Finally, after an eternity, the pain went and he straightened, heaving air into his lungs.

There was no need to check beneath the dressing gown. It had grown again; he could feel its weight threatening to drag him down. Stanton began to cry. He couldn't take it any longer. It wasn't fair. Nobody

deserved this, not for anything, certainly not for fooling around. Poor Tina. She had been right about that. And now he felt the same way as he had treated her. Like shit.

Stanton wiped his nose with the back of his hand, more determined than ever to find the doll. Glancing around him, though, he realised that might not be so easy. The shed was a jumble of bags and boxes and stacked newspapers. A lawnmower was propped up in one corner, wedged into place by an old kitchen stool. Against one wall, under the window, was a workbench which Stanton never used, more boxes stacked on its surface. He did not know where to start. His shoulders slumped in defeat. He would never find it, not in his condition. He turned to leave.

The doll hung from a nail on the door. Stanton knew he hadn't put it there, just as he knew he had not tied the string by which the doll was suspended. He reached out, noticing as he did so the small green shoot growing away from the bump at the base of the torso. It's her, the fucking old bitch. She's done something -

Silencing the voice in his head, Stanton grasped the doll, unhooked it from the nail. Why hadn't he noticed it on the way in?

He'd been frozen solid, that's why. No way the doll had suddenly appeared just for him to find. No such thing as magic, or whatever the hell it was Peggie Hall had worked on him. And he would prove it by cutting off the shoot. There was a pair of cutters in one of the workbench drawers. He rummaged around, found them, held them up to the light like a surgeon checking some vital instrument for dirt or flaws.

Then he picked up the doll. He was going to do it. His hands shook as he placed the shoot between the blades. Small details sprang into focus; the patterns in the wood that looked almost tiny carved runes, the way the shoot curved downwards, the fact that it was perceptibly growing even as he watched ...

Sweat broke out anew on his forehead. He did not notice it roll into his eyes, stinging. He was aware only of the doll, the source of all his misery. His palms were wet and he tightened his grip to prevent the cutters slipping. He had to do it now.

His nerve failed him. Almost sobbing with frustration, Stanton threw the cutters to the floor and raised the doll to his face.

It's you. Believe in it.

He shook his head angrily. It wasn't him, wasn't even a proper doll. Just a piece of wood, some twigs and a bit of string. He was ill, that was ill. He would have to make the journey back to the house, get help somehow. But then there was another surge of growth between his legs, so powerful it made the others feel like twinges. Everything went dark, and stayed that way even after he came to.

He was flat on his back, staring at the shed roof. Moonlight cast oddly-angled shadows across the wood. He tried to raise his head but did not have the strength. It was then that Stanton became aware of the heat between his legs. His right arm was a leaden weight when he lifted it; the left was dead. He touched

carefully. The Enemy was now almost the length of his leg and half as thick. It pulsed weakly but there was no pain. There were pins and needles in his hand and he realised he could not feel his extremities because too much blood was being drawn away from them.

For a moment he felt like weeping again, but then the feeling went away and he was empty. He reached for the doll while he still had the strength. It was right next to him. He raised it and studied it dispassionately. Even in the dim moonlight he could see the shoot was a vibrant green colour and that it had not stopped growing. He imagined sap pumping through it, giving life.

Stanton did not know where the cutters had fallen, so he opened his mouth and placed the shoot between his teeth. Then he bit down.

Smoke

Gary Greenwood

I smoke too much. I always gauged my cigarette intake by the stains on the index and middle fingers of my right hand, using my skin as a litmus paper guide to my addiction. Of course, I wanted to quit. But, of course, I never did.

Some smokers do give up the wonderful, filthy, antisocial habit when they realise it's killing them. At first, they smoke as if they will be forever young, not bothering to look to the future which lays in wait, a dark, heavy cloud laden with a rain of tumours. They believe they will be able to stop before the storm breaks over them. After they have stopped smoking, in the years to come, they believe they will have the umbrella of healthy eating and exercise to shield them from the black rain.

But by then, the damage is done.

I started when I was seventeen; a friend offered me a Marlboro as we sat drinking our beer in the local pub. I looked at the slim tube, the speckled filter pointing towards me, and thought, what the hell? Nothing more dramatic than that began the addiction which has stuck with me, non-stop, for thirteen years.

Thirteen years. Rather an apt number, I suppose. You see, I'm going to die. There's no doubt about that; which one gets me first is the only thing I'm taking bets on. Will it be the chronic lung cancer that sits on my chest, waking me every morning with a rattling cough as pieces of my flesh fall into my air ways, forcing me to hawk and spit and retch? Or the pancreatic cancer that sits quietly, seeming to do nothing to the odd organ in my belly that I have no idea why I need, and yet, I am told, is vital to my existence? Or will it be the clogged arteries around my heart, tumours constricting the flow of blood through my internal highways, tiny black traffic cones strangling the motion of the corpuscles?

No-one wants to take my bets. I'm offering good odds on all three diseases, yet none of my friends want to put any money down. I suppose I'm not surprised. I think it'll be the pancreas to go first, myself. If I didn't have that, the doctor told me they could probably cure the other two - a heart op for one, chemotherapy for the other. Trouble is, pancreatic cancer's terminal. No treatment, no cure. As I'm going to die anyway, they sent me home to while away my last few months. A counsellor calls around once a week to see how I'm doing, a man who has dealt with so many prospective corpses that he has ceased to view me as a human being. I am merely the loosely connected bag of bones sat in an armchair, an oxygen bottle and mask at my side like a forgotten child begging for attention.

The counsellor tells me that if the pancreatic cancer takes me away (his phrase) then chances are it will be quick and sudden. No pain, no fuss. One minute I'm a human being with a full set of experiences and memories that make me unique to this world, the next I'm a large collection of decaying cells. He doesn't quite put it like that, of course. Neither does he tell me that a heart attack or stroke will most likely be extremely painful and may leave me alive, yet disabled. Nor does he mention me spending my last few minutes on this earth coughing up the bloody, tattered vestiges of my beleaguered lungs, clumps and fronds of cancer coursing through the blood as it vomits from my mouth and nose.

But then, he isn't paid to tell me that.

My fingers, my litmus paper guides, are yellow. Trails of smoke have poured from between them over the years and, while I used to wash my hands in a bleach solution occasionally to rid myself of the marks, now I merely look at them, the badges of my addiction. If I hold out my hands, comparing right to left, there is a marked difference. The left, though the skin is drawn tight over the bones (cancer is a wonderful diet if nothing else) looks relatively normal. The right, however, is emblazoned by the yellow and brown stains that have sunk into the very creases of the skin, a painting built up over time by the lightest touch of a nicotine brush.

I'm at home now, ever since the kind doctors informed me that my pancreatic cancer cannot be treated. There was no sense in my taking up a bed which could be used to house a patient with a chance of recovery, so, as I say, I was sent home. My home. The few friends who still bother to visit me here complain with almost one voice that the place stinks of cigarette smoke. I merely shrug off their heckling, content in my little yellow world.

I believe I have come to terms with the fact that I am going to die. Not the idea, which most people think of at some point in their lives, but the actual fact that my life is going to end. There will be nothing left of me. Nothing. My last will and testament sits on the mantelpiece behind the small carriage clock my grandmother gave to me many years ago when I bought the house. Its glass dome cover is now thick with dust, the chimes broke some time ago, and I haven't wound it up since I came back from hospital. The smoke in the air taints even the envelope of my will, ageing it prematurely, the crisp, pristine white turning a sickly brown day by day, much like my body.

I'm going to die soon. I know that. I spend my time sitting here at my desk, idly typing verses and tales that no-one will read until I am gone, and, as strange as it may seem to someone else, I am content. I am ready.

There is no twist to the end of this rambling tale, no sting in this story. I am dying, that is a fact. I wish that I could, by typing the words "Reader, it is all a lie," make it so, but fiction is a poor substitute for reality. I have been tempted to wonder about alternate lives I could have lived, how things would have turned out if I had made different choices but I could not face an exploration into the uncharted realms of my life, the areas of my existence which might still have been had I not started smoking, had I not contracted cancer. That land would be too vivid, too full of the bright images that we keep in our heads and pretend are our memories, unaware that the dark patches of shadow that form our most painful experiences have been glossed over. Nobody cares to look at them, concentrating instead upon the good times that shine like tiny diamonds in a coal field. I could not travel there.

Instead, I shall sit here and, after I finish typing this, I shall reach into my pocket and take out a Marlboro and light it up. I will sit and watch as the sun sinks down to the horizon, peeping weakly through the clouds as I peer weakly through the smoke.

I shall sit, and I shall smoke, and I shall wait for one last visitor.

BLAC
eLevato
GOING
down

For past RazorBlade titles vist:

www.razorbladepress.com

Coming in 2002 From RazorBlade Press:

September – Heart by Simon Morden (ISBN 09542267 04 £4.99 $11.00)
                              -Raw Nerve 9 – Edired by Brian Willis

October - Cuckoo by Richard Wright (ISBN 09542267 71 £4.99 - $11.00)
              - Black Elevator Going Down by Chris Nurse

November – Scorpion by Brian Willis and Chris Poute (ISBN 09542267 47 £4.99 - $11.00)

December - The Percolated Stars by Rhys Hughes. (ISBN 09542267 12 £4.99 - $11.00)

Printed in the United Kingdom
by Lightning Source UK Ltd.
1019